TELLING
-TALES-

Robert Hanrott *&* Martha Horsley

Drawings by Martin Honeysett

B|Y|D
PRESS

Library of Congress Control Number: 2002106707

Set in Fairfield Light and Fenice Light
Typeset by P. M. Gordon Associates
Printed in the United States of America
by Thomson-Shore

ISBN 0-9721035-5-4

ByD Press

USA:

PO Box 3725
Washington DC 20007-2840
Tel/fax: (202) 342-0476

UK:
Flaxpool
Crowcombe TA4 4AW
Tel: 01984 618302

bydpress@erols.com

— Foreword —

We thought of the idea of "Telling Tales" on a walking holiday from Canterbury to Rome in the summer of 2000. The year 2000 was the six-hundredth anniversary of the death of Geoffrey Chaucer, whose characters in the *Canterbury Tales* traveled the medieval road from Southwark to Canterbury. What, we thought, if we continued that journey six hundred years later with a new and modern cast of characters, drawn from our imagination? They could walk on from Canterbury to Rome, following the old pilgrim route as we ourselves had done. And they could recount their own stories as Chaucer's characters did so many centuries ago.

Six hundred years apart, and what a different world! Yet traditional professions persist in modern guise, and age-old motivations still seem familiar. We cannot aspire to the genius of Chaucer (to whom we apologize, for we have taken the liberty to parody his verse); but we can, in our own way, comment on the vices, virtues and eccentricities of today's world. When all is said and done, human nature has changed but little. We therefore dedicate these tales to the memory of Geoffrey Chaucer (1342–1400), and trust that they will still seem relevant to our grandson, Henry Hanrott, when he's able to read them.

Our thanks to Morris Berman, Alex Christians, Jane and Martin Dean, Carmen Grayson, Martha Hoopes, Braxton Horsley, Frans Kok, Peter Porosky and Heddy Reid for their advice.

R.H. and M.H.
Washington, D.C., 2002

Contents

Prologue 1

THE TALES

Prologue

When in June the copious showers fall
And England sees no sign of sun at all;
And shivering tourists in their winter wear,
Wait for the warmth and practice solitaire;
And tennis fans in damp and mist do laze,
Read one more book, and their umbrellas raise;
And cricketers, their matches not begun,
Retire to the bar without a single run;
And hikers their extremities do rub
And, thankful, gather shivering in the pub;
And fishermen who cast upon the flood
Cycle home early, galoshes caked in mud;
And all that's left of Junes that used to be
Are summer berries, double cream, and tea;
Then serious people *"seek the stranger strands*
Of far-off saints, hallowed in sundry lands."
Ah! Chaucer! These your words do still apply;
Such witness to man's faith will never die.

Two thousand was, we know, the Holy Year,
When pilgrims flocked to Rome from far and near
And through the Holy Door did enter in
St. Peters, for the remission of their sin.
The indulgence was revived should they confess
To sins committed under modern stress.
And for committed Papal cognoscenti,

"Novo Millennio Ineunte."
No, Chaucer, nothing very much changed;
Religion as usual, slightly rearranged.

But now, twelve walkers with more mixed agendas,
Intrigued by the fame of Rome's refurbished splendors,
Seek in truth companionship and fun
(and wine), foregathering to enjoy the sun.
Imaginations roused, they think they'll shed
Some pounds by treading where the pilgrims tread.
No, not a march of faith, but still a cursory nod
To those who with more pious motives plod.
So come they forth for quite a lengthy walk,
At which some others, indolent, might balk:
"A walk through Europe? That is far too far!
How many miles? So why not go by car?"

Oh unromantic, hurried, weighty souls,
Cast in long-accustomed, anxious roles!
Let's face the truth: this journey's but a jape,
A mere excuse for what's a wise escape!
These walkers, free and leisured, have the time
(or think they do) to walk and talk and climb.
Forbearing to sit by and idly loll,
They lower, quickly, their cholesterol;
Leave children, traffic, phones, and daily care,
And on two pilgrim's feet in open air
They gaze at ruins and at Alpine flowers,
Walk Roman roads and forest tracks for hours.

Across the mountains, streams and fields they roam,
Walking the route from Canterbury to Rome!

Ah! Chaucer!
Chaucer's pilgrims journeyed down to Kent,
Recounting ancient stories as they went.
Six hundred years and ample history past,
We have a modern, if not wiser, cast
Of characters who somehow might reflect
The modern state of mind and intellect.
Instead of Southwark with its pungent air
To Canterbury our modern group repair;
And in an ancient inn they do convene
And talk of walking and of fine cuisine.
Then in Cathedral they all share a prayer,
Before next day they set out *en plein air,*
And to its beauty they do all succumb,
A taste of many *duomo*s yet to come.

So let us introduce you to our cast
Who, unlike Chaucer in the distant past,
Tell brand new tales, not those of ancient days,
To garner your approval, blame or praise.
Some are natives of the British Isles;
Some Americans have flown for miles.
For some a hoard of money's their pursuit,
For power, control, for influence and repute.
Others are gurus, known as "soul artistes,"
Who've largely taken over from the priests.

Some are steadfast pillars of the land,
Making work whatever comes to hand.
And, lastly, those with public sex appeal,
Tarred with that brush, however they might feel.
Rejecting coach, the train, and aerodrome,
They walk the route from Canterbury to Rome.

Evelyn, a surgeon, oozing wealth;
Darryl, a trainer, here in muscled health;
Nigel, practitioner of British law;
And Colonel Gerald, former man of war.
Moira, with her counselor's listening ear;
And Alan, investment banking's his career.
Meet Nicola with her herbal regimen
And Lizzie, with a roving eye for men.
All gaze at Randall, the Adonis of the Jet;
How godlike can an airline pilot get?
There's Richard, merchant, balding, slightly fat;
And lastly Shirley, clever bureaucrat.
These hikers, all with winter's pallid skin,
Foregather at the ancient Falstaff Inn,
Some their disrupted lives to re-deploy;
Some an exciting venture to enjoy.

Wary introductions are begun;
First impressions are not soon undone.
Nigel, the lawyer, offers up a toast.
(This Nigel, garrulous, expatiates the most.)
"To sun and wine, companionship and Rome,

And good, tall tales we can re-tell at home."
And they respond: "To wine and safe arrival,"
And, smiling, pray for blisterless survival.
Nigel proposes: "As we walk along,
From each of us a yarn, not over-long,
Illumining our lives, and of a scale
No more prolix than a Chaucerian tale.
We'll honor, thus, the poet, and I think
It complements the French cuisine and drink."

"A good idea," said one, "but I'm concerned.
He who bares his soul can then get burned.
In Middle English too? That's for the birds!
In any case, I have forgot the words!"
"Good point," another said, "but even worse,
Were we to tell our modern tales in verse."
And up speaks Nigel, ever organizing,
"There's no intention to be tyrannizing.
Don't fret, speak prose, avoid all complication,
Besides, there is no fear of publication.
Just do not bore us, or you're on your own,
No dull accounts, like "Audits I Have Known!"
Let muse, imagination both take flight
And, truth or fiction, let them both delight.
And unlike Chaucer, who retold known tales,
Let's be ambitious, though on smaller scales.
Think of our pasts, excitements we have known,
Daydream or nightmare, even overblown.
Speak of ourselves, or failing that, a friend,

But once past the climax, quickly make an end.
Ah! One last thing before you all commence
Your wisdom and experience to dispense:
However many you are speaking to
Whether to all the group or just a few,
Don't interrupt with comment or aside;
Words picked with care are said with pride.
Your turn will come, let him enjoy his glory,
Be quiet and courteous. And now, begin a story!"

– The Plastic Surgeon's Tale –

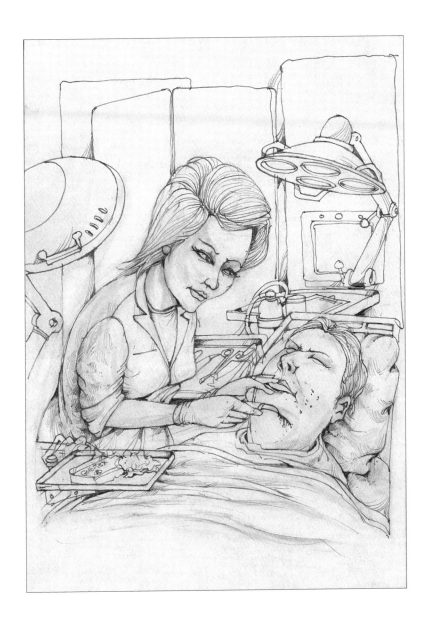

Evelyn

She sells her solace in the riper years;
Working her wonders, the wrinkle disappears.
Eternal life she offers! (Well, the truth:
A brief reversion to a bygone youth.)
A short, assertive blonde, dressed all in black,
With Gucci scarf, designer anorak,
No errant crease or hemline out of place
Or hint of age to score a perfect face.
Her lovely legs do men's libido rouse;
She has a gold insignia on her blouse.
And Oh! That flawless figure, and those eyes
(Well, in this business you must advertise!)
Engender faith; yet gain dictates her life.
Ruthless she is with laser and with knife.
Self-confident, the laws of luck she flouts,
But depth of makeup hides some nagging doubts.

"Oh, leave me alone, can't you?" snapped Evelyn at the street vendor, as she emerged from the cathedral courtyard and walked through the morning street market, scarcely noticing the clothing and baby jumpers swinging in the breeze.

Moira, the counselor, and Nicola, the herbalist, had accompanied Evelyn through the cathedral nave, pausing in the Chapel of St. Anselm before setting out along the Pilgrim's Way from Canterbury towards Dover. Clearly, the peace of the little chapel had done little to calm Evelyn's nerves. This was not a good start to a morning's walk.

"I'm sorry," said Evelyn, noticing the look of alarm on the faces of her companions. A single tear rolled down her cheek, leaving a furrow in the rouged powder. "I guess my nerves are on edge. I'm here on vacation, trying to relax. But just standing there in the chapel brought it all back to me. It all seems so unfair!"

"Would you like to talk about it? We can see you're upset."

Moira's professional interest was piqued. This could be the first of the tales. It had been the idea of Nigel, the lawyer, that each person tell a story, either to the group as a whole or to just one or two members.

"Yes, perhaps I would like to talk about it, but just to you two. I'd rather not discuss it in front of the whole group."

"Take your time."

Evelyn smoothed her hair as she collected herself. Mascara smudged the simple cotton handkerchief she withdrew from the pocket of her anorak.

"It's about Henry, my husband," she began. "You never know about people, do you? The truth is, I *made* Henry. He was a farm boy. Without me he'd be digging rutabagas in Nowheresville. I was his passport out of Iowa, and he couldn't get out quickly enough.

"I met Henry in college. He was leaving the Dean's office just as I was going in, and he held the door for me. He was tall and slim, with merry eyes, and he seemed to look on the world with silent amusement. He wanted to talk about Updike and Bellow and Mailer. I suppose I never took that seriously. I did most of the talking, but then I had the most to say.

"Later on, after the first rush, I realized he wasn't what you'd call good looking. His face was pockmarked from acne, and he had a receding chin that just sort of dropped away as if it had never been properly finished. But he had a good sense of humor and he was a good listener. In those days I wanted to be an actress, and Henry would stay up late at night to help me learn my lines. I worshipped Garbo and Dietrich and toyed with the idea of the New York stage, but my father was dead set against it. 'I haven't paid for your college education to watch you hoofing on 42nd Street. No money in that!' Money was big in our house. If people had household shrines, ours would have held a framed hundred-dollar bill.

"So I went to medical school. Henry and I moved in together, and he seemed to be happy with that arrangement. It was understood that we'd get married, and eventually we did. Henry was easy to be with, and I knew he'd be a good right-hand man who wouldn't play around. You can do worse, you know.

"I went through my internship and residency and obtained my certification from the American Board of Plastic Surgery and a Craniofacial Fellowship. Then I taught in New Jersey for a couple of years and performed minor surgeries on the side, but I wanted to make money. So I interviewed in California and bought into a big practice with a stellar reputation in Burbank.

"'Why Burbank?' Henry asked. 'If we're going to California, why not San Francisco or Santa Barbara?'

"'Burbank's right next to Hollywood,' I explained. 'People in Hollywood need to look good, and that's my business. You could write TV and movie scripts. Hollywood's the place; you just have to meet the right people.'

"So off we went to Burbank. Henry got a job teaching English at a local community college. His job paid for the groceries, but I was earning most of the money. Henry became a house husband, since his hours were short. He kept up the place and later on supervised the housekeeper, who also did the cooking. When I came home from the clinic, there'd be a meal on the table for me.

"I joined the Burbank practice at a good time. The group had a flourishing clientele, but they were almost all women. The male market was largely untapped, but had a huge potential. Men couldn't get top jobs in big companies unless they looked the part, regardless of management ability, or even intelligence. The look had to be neat, sleek, strong, and square-jawed. Ambitious middle executives were gazing at themselves in the mirror, noticing their sagging jowls, and beginning to use their annual leave for cosmetic surgery. Boomers were flocking in for rhinoplasties.

"The senior partner chose me to go after the male clients partly because I was a woman. And having a pretty face helped when I was persuading someone to spend his money. I think image and presentation are ninety percent of success, don't you?"

Evelyn paused a moment and took a compact from the pocket of her anorak. She gazed attentively in the mirror, admiring her skin, and used the puff to dab delicately at the tear-stains under her eyes. "And no, I haven't had a rhytidectomy. Not yet. But can you see this little squint mark up here, between the eyebrows? I need to do something about it. Can you see it in this light?"

The three women stopped while Moira and Nicola searched Evelyn's face for the offending wrinkle.

Evelyn continued. "Our practice has its own clinic, equipped with the latest operating and monitoring instruments, including a Coherent CO_2 Ultra Pulse Laser, a flash scanner, and computer imaging, all that."

Moira and Nicola looked impressed.

"As part of my deal with the senior partner, I got the new extension that was built on a former children's playground at the rear of the clinic, so my patients could enter discreetly. Most men are reluctant to reveal their vanities.

"I used my own money to decorate my consulting rooms, with no expense spared. We had a faux-log fire, deep carpets and sofas upholstered in fabrics with hunting scenes. Some practices went for ultramodern, but I preferred the country gentleman look, like a London men's club. I hired a low-paid actress with a husky voice as a receptionist and had her wear a short dress. First impressions count. And I recruited an aesthetician. Bambi was twenty-five and stunning when she joined me. She'd been Miss Nevada before getting certified in dermatech-permanent cosmetics. She does the facials and makeup. Oh yes, makeup for men! Believe me!

"We run the business together. I do the surgery, Bambi the styling. The receptionist doubles as a manicurist. I now have a part-time hair stylist and an apparel consultant who worked for Ralph Lauren in Italy. The hair stylist advises on facial hair styles and the scalp problems that middle-aged men get, in addition to doing the usual cuts and perms. He teams with the glow colorist, the dental perfection consultant, and the perfect sight specialist. Glasses aren't sexy any longer unless they're tinted; our clients can choose from twenty tints.

"When required, we bring in a sex therapist. Men who come to us often find that their image problems are affecting their sex lives. You can't always separate the two things. Sometimes it's the fading sex drive that makes them think about cosmetic surgery. Of course, Viagra has simplified things considerably, and we can prescribe it as long as we consult their primary physician.

"We also have a dietician and an alternative medicine specialist on call, and a list of gyms we recommend. Look, we're rejuvenating the whole man! No point in surgery if you still have a forty-four inch waist, boring glasses and a sallow complexion. We want our clients to feel good about themselves; then they'll look good to other people. Besides, cosmetic surgery is primarily for people who have a healthy lifestyle, exercise regularly, and don't smoke or drink to excess. Our strategy is for the client to diet and get fit, spruce up his image, then last of all have surgery and facial treatments. The new man emerges gradually, but it's a holistic approach.

"We have a fixed-fee schedule for the surgery, and I collect overhead on the other services. It works well, and it's the only full-service, one-stop, male, physical-image-consulting outfit in California. I call it Resur-rection®. Reassurance, erection— get it? Here's my card. If you have a male friend, tell him to call. Trudi, the receptionist, will fix up a complimentary consultation to talk to him about his lifestyle and his goals for himself over the next twenty years. We have people coming from as far away as Sydney, Australia, believe me! Think about it."

Moira and Nicola each inspected the card and tucked it away safely.

"Now, the senior partner may have taken me on to attract some male clients, but I had another agenda. I still loved the theater and the movies and I adored the gossip columns. I knew who was divorcing whom, who had bought a beachside mansion, and who had which part in which movie. I always dreamed of mixing with the stars and discussing the intimate details of their lives.

"Well, today it's all about personalities, image and status, who you know and what you have. Nobody thanks you for being poor. That's why there are so many people in this country who become workaholics. Look at the personalities in *People* and *Entertainment Weekly*! They're the ones who've made it. We're all trying to grab a part of it, if we can. Why not?

"As head of Resur-rection®, I go to all the cocktail parties, barbecues, opening nights and so on. It's great. I'm recognized by the paparazzi and gossip columnists. One magazine recently called me 'face-saver to the stars.' I've been a guest on radio and TV talk shows, and I've been featured in all the top men's journals. I get the stardom without the boredom. Henry used to say that going to all these events was my real vocation."

Evelyn paused once again and applied a touch of Yves St.-Laurent Musk Ox Lip Toner, while admiring the silky bounce of her hair, care of l'Oréal.

"Ah yes, I was telling you about Henry, wasn't I? Well, when Henry wasn't teaching, he liked to read and write. His den in the back of the house was full to the ceiling with novels, poetry, biographies, and magazines. I tried to get him to keep his books on shelves or in neat piles on the floor, but he wasn't receptive to the idea. I also tried to get him to come to some of the parties. It wasn't good for him to spend so much time at home by himself, reading or preparing his lectures. I thought the least he could do was to help the business by talking it up, doing a little customer recruitment. But when I introduced him at a party, the person would look over Henry's shoulder to see if there was someone more important around. Henry usually ended up in a corner somewhere drinking by himself—drinking too much, usually. We argued about it. I felt he was letting me down.

"Then, one day, at some event—oh, I remember; it was Gwyneth Paltrow's Oscar nomination party. I was in the ladies' room, and I overheard a conversation between two young women, starlets probably, or friends of the hostess.

"One said to the other: 'She's smart and attractive, too. I hope I look that good when I'm her age (*jeez, I'm only forty-four!*). But that husband of hers is gross! I can't look at him without wanting to vomit. There should be a law against chins like that. And she's a plastic surgeon! You know, he cornered me this evening and started bending my ear about existentialism. You gotta be joking! I can't even spell it!'

"It was then that I began to realize I had to do something about Henry. You know, I didn't really notice him much. I mean, really *notice* him. Back when we were dating, I thought: *Who cares about looks? He's got a brain and we get along. He's probably going into teaching, he doesn't need to be a photographic model.* And after that, I guess I just didn't pay much attention."

"How was it with Henry? I mean, sexually?" asked Moira. Nicola, whose own attention had been flagging while Evelyn enthused about her business, now looked at Evelyn expectantly. This was more like it.

"Occasionally I had the energy for sex, but I preferred it in the dark, fantasizing about the latest movie stud. Usually Henry was too boozed to last more than a minute or so, and that was that. But at least he didn't take ecstasy. Ecstasy's stupid. You know, it's going around all over Hollywood, but there's where I part company. When you have a business to run, as I do, you can't get into that.

"Anyway, Henry eventually stopped teaching. His college was downsizing and he said he wanted to write more anyway. I said it would be okay, as long as he continued to run the house. That was only fair. And he was supportive, I'll give him that. He upgraded the computer system at the clinic for me. He could make an effort if he wanted to.

"I knew Henry always wanted to write. But how many people make money writing fiction? One in a million? When we first arrived in Burbank, he took some scriptwriting classes and actually got a couple of spec TV scripts read. Then he lost his enthusiasm. I suppose I didn't help. He would give me his stuff to look at, but I never had the time. I was working my ass off.

"But I really had to do something about his looks. His receding chin and discolored, pockmarked skin were real turnoffs. He was a liability to my practice. If I couldn't make my own husband look good, I shouldn't be in the business, right? The problem was how to raise the subject. I knew the direct approach was out. *Henry, if you're coming with me to these glamorous events, we've got to do something about your looks.* I'm no psychologist, but I knew that wouldn't do.

"So I thought up this strategy, a sort of 'softly, softly catchee monkey' approach. First, I'd get him more at ease in company; he was still hanging around on the sidelines.

"'Henry, darling, I need your help on these social occasions. You're a smart guy. No, really, you are. All these extroverts, posing and showing off, it's hard to get a word in edgewise. You have interesting things to say, and you've got a great sense of humor. What about a course in public speaking? It would do wonders for your self-image.' Henry agreed, reluctantly, and I enrolled him in a local toastmaster's course. After that, he talked more, and started expressing stronger opinions on a whole range of things, from how much we paid the house-keeper to what flavor of coffee we bought. So far, so good.

"The second stage of the strategy was health. His drinking worried me, and his potbelly, too. So I got him to join my gym; that way we could work out together. At first, he complained, but I arranged for a personal trainer to get him going. I picked a young, good-looking Chinese woman named Sheila to keep him focused. I took her aside and shared my concerns.

"'If he's fit, he'll feel better about himself. And if he feels better about himself, maybe he'll stop drinking.'

"Sheila got the point and put Henry through his paces, while smiling, flirting a bit, and teasing him about his flabby pecs. It seemed to do the trick, and he started staying longer at the gym, working the upper body machines and watching features on the individual monitor as he burned calories on the treadmill. His weight went down, and his clothes began to look baggy. I took him shopping and made sure he bought a snappy outfit. Look, image was my job! Bambi came with us and that cheered him up, although, I must say, I think she overdid it a bit.

"'Henry, that suit is fabulous. It really looks great on you. Care for a date, handsome?' She laughed and displayed her perfect teeth. I had never thought about Bambi using her powers of persuasion on *my* husband. But she was helpful.

"'You look terrific, Henry.' Bambi told him. 'Those shoes are awesome. I'm just a little worried about the hair.'

"'What the hell's wrong with my hair, goddamn it, apart from the fact that it's falling out?' said Henry.

"'Why don't you try to shorten it a bit round the back, sweep the sides back and put the part nearer the middle? Look!' And with a few flicks of a comb, Bambi transformed Henry's hair.

"Before I knew it, Henry looked quite the European man around town, snappily dressed, well groomed, and glowing with health. But, that chin! Henry was ready for the *coup de grâce,* the final transformation.

"'I married one of the best-looking men in California, potentially,' I said to Henry. Yes, it was a lie, but a white one.

"'Potentially?'

"'Look!' I said, grabbing a mirror and using my hand to cover up his apology for a chin, with its loose skin drooping below it.

"'I get it, you want to stick me with a new chin. Well, I'm *not* a movie star, never will be. You married this model and you're stuck with it.'

"'Please, Henry. Everything else is perfect! Just give it a try. Most men would be delighted to be transformed at your age. John Wayne had a couple of facelifts, and Marilyn Monroe had a chin implant. You'd look rugged and handsome and ten years younger if you'd agree.'

"Well, I usually get what I want. It's unfair, but life's unfair! What was I to do, get a new husband?"

"Were you ever tempted?" Nicola asked.

"Frankly, I was too busy to think much about it. And I'm not stupid, you know. Where else would I find someone as easy going as Henry? The alternative would probably be some ego-freak whose job was more important than mine and who had affairs all over town. No, I didn't want to swap him for anyone else, not really. It was just that chin!

"I won the battle, and a date was set for his surgery. I don't get many mentoplasties, so this was a little out of the ordinary. Basically, it's a bit like a breast enhancement operation in that you're padding out the chin with synthetic material, in this case Gore-tex, the membrane used to make hiking clothes weatherproof. Honestly! It's flexible, soft, and very strong. In fact, you can carve the plastic, what they call 'subcutaneous augmentation material,' into the exact shape you want. The trick is to eliminate the receding chin while making the throat skin look natural. Nothing gives away age more than the neck and throat, and yet a chin job looks obvious if the skin is taut. You have to watch it. Implants can get infected or slip out of position, which is embarrassing, although Gore-tex has been used for thirty years and is very reliable. It encourages natural tissue ingrowth, too. That's why I use it. Occasionally implants can also damage the sensation of the lower lip, although my patients never have that problem.

"I also did a laser treatment on Henry's face. You have to be careful with lasers; burn too deep and you're in all sorts of trouble. There's some preparation to do, but the procedure only takes a few minutes, and I thought, why not? Oh, and I gave Henry a Botox injection to reduce his brow frown lines. It has to be done again every three to six months, but that's all right."

"He had the whole works, then?" Although winded, Moira strained to keep abreast of the other two women on the uphill climb.

"Not the whole works. What I could get away with. I hadn't told him in advance about the skin resurfacing. Anyway, I was pleased with the results. His chin came out well: firm and determined, but not too prominent. Just a slight hint of a cleft and a nice, straight jaw. The skin around the throat was loose enough to look natural, but taut enough to look youthful. I was proud of the job, really proud."

"I bet you were," said Nicola. "Was Henry pleased?"

"If he was, he didn't show it. For several weeks, of course, he couldn't move his jaw and could only drink liquids. It must have been uncomfortable for him. But when he felt better, we opened a bottle of champagne to celebrate. 'To our new life,' I said, although I hardly got a smile out of him. Henry just shrugged his shoulders.

"But it *was* a new life. I could tell that people, especially women, were looking at Henry in a new way. I had reinvented him, but I hadn't thought about the consequences. It was shortly afterwards, at the preview of a Brad Pitt movie. I was just chatting with Paul (Newman, that is), and out of the corner of my eye I spotted Henry in deep conversation with a blonde in a cheetah-skin outfit. Some Australian actress, I think. Well, women used to look bored when they were talking to Henry. They'd just stare at their feet or turn away as if to say 'just got to go.' This woman had Henry in a corner and looked as if she were about to rape him. Her arms supported her against the walls on either side of his shoulders, trapping him. I excused myself and went to the rescue. He was supposed to be focusing on the men, talking about golf or yachting, and encouraging them to contact me, spend their money, and rejuvenate themselves. I told him so.

"'There's no point coming to these parties, Henry, if you waste your time talking to young people who won't need surgery for ten years.'

"Well, after that Henry didn't show much interest in social events and came to fewer parties. That seemed to suit him fine. But leaving him at home alone wasn't such a good idea, either. He was the same Henry, but better looking and more composed. People were taking an interest in him for the first time in our marriage. He'd get calls at the house. Sometimes the phone would ring, and the person calling would hang up when I answered. And once a woman left a message saying how much she'd enjoyed the first chapter of his novel, and how beautifully he wrote. I thought, *First chapter? I didn't even know he was writing a novel!*

"I wasn't jealous or anything, but I bought myself a couple of new at-home lounge suits, one in chartreuse and another in ice-blue. And I had my hair bobbed in the back. Shorter hair makes a woman look younger, if she's over forty. What I was losing in youth, I could gain in style. I knew I had to revive our marriage. It seemed to have dried in the air, like French bread. And it was going to stay that way, stale I mean, if we hardly ever saw each other. I had been the workaholic all those years, after all, and I felt it was my responsibility to do something. So I decided to spend more time at home and less time at the clinic. It didn't make sense to leave Henry with all that free time.

"I remember the first day I came home early. I found Henry hunched over in the den, writing furiously. There were discarded papers everywhere. I got him to clean up the mess and come into town with me on an errand. I was walking down the street with him and you could see the women, even quite young ones, giving him the eye. We stayed downtown and had dinner at a nice place I had always wanted to go to. An actor from 'Friends' was there with a gorgeous redhead; I was surprised Henry could keep his eyes off her.

"Anyway, soon after that, the trouble began. Henry retreated more and more into the den, shutting the door, even on weekends. He stopped planning the meals, so I had to supervise the housekeeper. At first I didn't mind so much. Henry usually arranged for a meat-and-potatoes-style main course with a dessert, whereas I like to have three light courses — lots of salads and a fruit dessert. Also, I put out the silver and the candles and insisted we take our time. I wanted our meals together to be special. But the minute dinner was over, Henry was back in the study.

"And then there was the pool. Henry had always kept the pool clean and supplied with the necessary chemicals, but algae started to appear. I got rather irritated with him and said, 'There's no point in having a pool if we don't keep it up. And the grass hasn't been cut in a month!' Henry had always enjoyed riding on our big mower, but he said he didn't have time anymore. I had to find a blow-and-mow service.

"It was really getting to be too much. I was still working most of the day at the clinic and then going home and having to take on all the chores. I felt frustrated; it didn't seem fair. Bambi suggested that we take a break, to relax and reconnect. 'You two haven't had a real vacation for years! The clinic will survive without you for two weeks.'

"So, I put it to Henry. 'Two weeks!' he replied, as if I had suggested two years.

"'Look,' I said, 'you sort through all those press cuttings of yours and choose a good hotel in a quiet resort with a decent beach.' But he never did.

"Then three months ago Henry left me altogether—psychologically, that is. Physically he's at home, but he may as well not be. I'm around more, but I see him less. He retreats into his den and just appears for meals. Part of the time he reads Calvino and Naipaul and Hornby, and part of the time he works on his novel. He's doing what he wants to do, but that spark he had when he was young has disappeared. And if I try to have a conversation with him, he says he can't talk, or he'll lose his train of thought.

"I wait up for him at night but fall asleep before he comes to bed. And when I get up in the morning, he's dead to the world. Sometimes he doesn't even make it upstairs. He just crashes on the couch in the living room. I find him there in the morning, surrounded by his papers, mugs of stale coffee, and ashtrays full of cigarette butts. Oh yes, Henry started smoking—he says it helps him concentrate. It stinks up the whole house, and I'm sure he knows I hate it. But I don't want to give him an excuse to leave.

"You see, I've been with Henry since I was eighteen. I really haven't known any other men intimately, and I don't know what I'd do without him. I forced myself to come on this trip without him. It's the first time I've been away from Henry since we were married. But it's actually easier than living in the same house with him and being ignored."

"I can understand that," said Moira. "How do you feel about the way he's behaving?"

Evelyn picked her way carefully along the chalk track in her stylish walking shoes, avoiding errant pieces of flint.

"I'm frightened. I still expect to meet Henry's glance and see the husband I married, and when I don't, I feel terribly alone. And then I get angry. All those years, building up the business, to get where we are. The house, the neighborhood, the pool. He couldn't have done that by himself, not as a college teacher."

Nicola glanced tentatively at Moira and then back at Evelyn.

"Is there another woman?" she asked.

"I don't *think* so. But I'm really worried about this novel of his. If it's a success, who knows . . . ?"

"Perhaps it's a phase. He'll get over it and get back in touch, emotionally."

"Unlikely. It's been three months now."

Nicola held out a handkerchief, and Evelyn took it gratefully.

"And I gave him so much."

"Maybe you've given him *too* much," said Moira. "He's asserting his independence. He now has the confidence. And he may feel resentful."

"Resentful? Why should he feel resentful?"

"Perhaps the best thing is to leave him alone for the time being," said Moira.

"Maybe I should have left him as he was," Evelyn murmured.

- The Investment Banker's Tale -

Alan

Here's a man who learned the City game,
To make a pile of money was his aim.
Persistently he realized his dream:
"From lukewarm gruel to strawberries and cream."
People are not his thing, it is his vice
To revel in r.o.c. and market price;
And if at an evening meal your eyes should meet,
He'll look beyond you to a balance sheet.
Never relaxing, in a field he'll stand,
A Palm Pilot held in steady, outstretched hand:
"Is it a dying dog, or can it fly?"
An e-mail sent via satellite through the sky.
Is greed the motivation of his life?
Must he compete to satisfy his wife?
No, it is neither, it is fear of pain,
Of losing all and being poor again.

"Where were you during the crossing?" asked Richard, as he braced himself against the June north wind and observed the lights of England across a foam-flecked Channel.

"Oh, I just walked across," replied Alan, who had agreed to go for an evening stroll along the sand dunes of Wissant with Richard, the small businessman, and Randall, the airline pilot. "I ruined a good pair of shoes."

"It's going to be one of those trips, is it?" Richard grinned at the City humor.

"Actually, I found a quiet place to check my e-mails," confessed Alan, gazing out to sea.

Richard followed Alan's gaze. "It makes you wonder how Julius Caesar ever got his army into England across this choppy stretch of water."

"Or how the famous Archbishop Sigeric made it in one of those flimsy medieval boats," added Randall.

Sigeric, a tenth-century Archbishop of Canterbury, landed in Wissant on his pilgrimage to Rome to collect his palium from the Pope. On the return trip, he kept a diary describing his route. We were traveling in his footsteps.

That night, Alan lay awake, reflecting on his walk among the dunes. The lights of England had reminded him of his outing on the Solent several months before, an outing that had given his life new direction. In the morning, his pale, clean-shaven face showed off the puffy bags beneath his eyes.

Alan joined Richard and Randall, and the three men set off together, ahead of the rest of the group, on the ancient Via Francigena. Randall tied his cashmere scarf tightly around his neck as protection against the brisk sea breeze. Before them were fields of wheat, mustard, and linseed oil, with church spires on the horizon. Alan had decided to share his story. He spoke with the slight estuary accent typical of South East England.

"I was reminded last night of a sailing trip I went on earlier this spring. I'll tell you about it, if you like."

Richard and Randall agreed. This idea of telling stories might be a good way to get to know the other walkers.

"I was invited to go sailing in the Channel by a fellow merchant banker, called Simon. Everyone in the business knew Simon. We had met at banking events, in hotel bars or meeting rooms, usually among a noisy crowd of people. Our conversation was the typical edgy shop talk of business acquaintances and competitors. We had never spent one-on-one time together.

"Simon was the golden boy of his bank. Well, 'boy' was pushing the envelope somewhat. Like myself, he was in his forties. His investment banking division was large and his opinions on economic trends and pet market sectors were quoted in the press. Part of Simon's success was his store of investment banking jokes. He not only remembered them, he made them up. His best deals were closed in upscale restaurants or private clubs, where he was reputed to drink even hardened alcoholics under the table. I was a bit nervous about the day's outing but told myself that at least I'd enjoy the jokes.

"Simon had his boat moored at Itchenor. Itchenor is one of a handful of villages along the length of Chichester Harbor, an estuary whose mouth lies opposite the Isle of Wight. The Romans were supposed to have landed their elephants on those tidal shores, the huge animals sinking in the gray oozy mud. The sailing is good, and its proximity to London makes the harbor popular with yachtsmen. Simon had a forty-eight foot fiberglass sloop moored in the center of what locals called the 'river,' opposite the Itchenor Sailing Club. With the aid of a dinghy and an outboard motor, we approached the yacht, which lay low and sleek, facing into the prevailing westerly wind.

"'Can we sail this, just the two of us?' I asked, with some anxiety. I knew the basics of sailing and loved being out on the water. But the idea of shinning up a mast in any sort of wind, let alone a Channel westerly, did not appeal.

"'Not a problem,' Simon replied. 'It's all mechanized these days. I have radar, satellite navigation, ship-to-shore radio, electric winches, and sails furled by power. I even have a hose that cleans the mud off the anchor chain as you weigh it. Sit back, enjoy it.'

"Lowering on the horizon were dark clouds that melded almost seamlessly into the gray mud flats. But in Chichester Harbour, the sun shone in a cloudless sky as we motored the four miles to the harbor entrance.

"'It's boring beating into the wind on this stretch,' said Simon. 'I always cheat. Like a drink?'

"We sat in the comfortable cockpit, single malts in hand for warmth against the fresh breeze. Simon glanced from time to time at his e-mails arriving on the satellite-linked computer by his elbow. You can gauge the importance attached to a conversation by whether your companion's mobile is turned on or off. Simon's was, mercifully, off. A good start, I thought, as I secretly disabled my own.

"'It's nice to have a chance to get to know you,' said Simon.

"'Likewise,' I replied. 'Thanks for the invitation.' I tried to sound relaxed.

"'I hear you're an oarsman,' said Simon.

"'Yes, thanks to the British Navy. I had a scholarship to Dartmouth.'

"'Keep it up?'

"'No, not really. My last race was a coxless pair at Henley, three years ago. And you?'

"'Golf, when I'm not working. You enjoy what you do well.' Two cockerels strutting, staking out their territory. 'Tell me about your operation.'

"So I told him. 'We started with five stock and bond traders. We now have a staff of fifty, after ten years. The investment banking division has been the most profitable, M & A work and IPOs.'

"'Tough business.'

"'I call myself Chief Beggar and I call the junior staff Nurse-maids. Once they identify a good start-up, I put out my bowl and beg for money. Frankly, it's not my favorite job. When it works, I get a buzz. When it doesn't, I feel like an Albanian peasant standing outside Waterloo Station with my cap out at rush hour.' This was my effort to sound light hearted.

"'Begging's my specialty,' said Simon, 'but the cash can come from unexpected sources. I brought a small engineering outfit to market a couple of years ago. At first no one would touch it. Then I went to an event at my old college and got chatting to someone at dinner. Used to go to tutorials with him at Magdalene. Next day he looks at the figures, announces it's just the thing for his portfolio, and insists it needs 250K not 100K. That deal returned fifty "X" in eighteen months.'

"'Great old boys' network,' I said, envious. But I don't think he heard me against the rising wind. He signaled for me to take the wheel for a moment, while he uncovered the mainsail and checked the jib sheets. It seemed to be a closeout on the conversation, but I was not to be outdone. Rivalry was the game of the moment, so I countered.

"'We underwrote a themed coffee shop last year. When trading opened, the shares were two hundred percent oversubscribed.'

"'You know old Marston at Begram Investments?' Simon asked.

"'I know *of* him, of course.'

"'Apparently the guy's such a workaholic he never moves from his desk. Afraid he'll miss a chance to make a buck. He tries to save time by not urinating. He's passed out twice from urea poisoning sitting right there at his desk!'

"We both laughed, but my mind was on other things."

At that moment Alan, Randall and Richard arrived at a paved road that crossed their dirt track. Intent on his tale and forgetting that he was in France, Alan looked to his right as he stepped onto the road and was nearly struck by a speeding car coming from the opposite direction.

"Damn lunatic!" he shouted.

Randall and Richard caught up with Alan and waited for him to regain his composure. After a few moments he continued:

"So I said to Simon, 'You're not too exposed to the high-tech sector. I guess you got that right.'

"'We're not a casino.' Simon steered towards the whitecaps beyond the narrows. *Was he trying to suggest we were too gung-ho?* I thought I had better respond.

"'Look, I don't throw money around and don't encourage others to,' I said, and changed the subject. 'I understand you're married.'

"'Yes, to a *very* busy lady,' Simon replied. 'She tells people she doesn't work, but in fact she never stops. This committee, that committee, chairman or secretary to half a dozen charities. Works informally with the Prime Minister's wife. They were at school together.'

"I could see he was being friendly, trying to take me into his confidence. It looked promising. 'You go to Downing Street, then?'

"'From time to time,' he replied nonchalantly, as if to say, *doesn't everybody?* 'We saw him in Tuscany not too long ago. No politics, just a general chat about the world at large.'

"Just a general chat about the world at large! Bloody poseur, I thought. I knew from the gossip that his wife's father was a wealthy industrialist whose company was quoted on the FT index. There was no doubt about Simon's connections.

"We had cleared the harbor mouth, and he turned the boat into the wind to raise mainsail and genoa. In older boats, this is when the crew usually springs into action, hauling and belaying. We remained in the cockpit as Simon fiddled impatiently with the switches and stared up at the pennant at the head of the mast. The wind was getting up. I noticed he had not fully raised the mainsail; it was effectively reefed. But we were under sail.

"'Tell me about your children,' I said. I wanted to capitalize on our rapport, get him to think I'd be a sympathetic colleague. I also wanted to keep some control over the conversation. I'd get nothing more than a salt-and-sea tan if I let him ask all the questions.

"'Ah, the girls. The older one's the serious one, writes historical novels and works for a publisher. The middle one's looking at her options, and the little one's finishing school in June.' He seemed a little guarded, and I noticed a tense look flit across his otherwise confident face. I thought it best not to press him.

"'You married?' he asked.

"'Yes, second time round,' I offered. 'My wife's just made a film, called *Waltz in the Dark.* That's the title in Britain, anyway. It's a low budget movie, but we're hoping to get a distributor in the States. My wife's stage name is Dorothy Blayne, if you're into the theater.' Got him! I could see he was impressed.

"'Children?'

"'Yes, two. Both with my first wife. My son's up at Oxford, trying out for an eight next weekend. Still competing with Dad. Need a summer whiz kid in your office?' I asked jokingly, and got no response. 'My girl just got four "A's" on her A levels. She'll have her pick of universities.' That seemed to take the wind out of his sails. And I was beginning to wish something would take the wind out of the sails above my head. It was getting choppy, and that cockpit seat was hard!

"'Get much sailing in these days?' I asked him, raising my voice over the wind and trying to regain the initiative.

"'Not much,' he replied. 'I've been spending time with punters on the nineteenth hole. And I play in a tournament about once a month. Took a team to Portugal and Spain earlier in the year.'

"Christ! This guy operates at the top of everything. The tally had lurched in his direction.

"By this time we were sailing westwards up the Solent, close-hauled into the wind. I emptied my third glass of single malt and, as Simon called for us to go about, I changed sides a bit unsteadily. Despite the shelter offered by land on either side of us, the sea was flecked with foam and a bank of angry clouds was approaching. A small fleet of racing boats scudded around us and disappeared into the shelter of Cowes.

"Simon gestured at the elements. 'Hope you don't get sick, old chap. The forecast was moderate gale, but you said this was a good day for you to come out. I doubt it'll be that bad.'

"'Don't worry about me,' I said, as Simon settled the boat onto a port tack. 'I guess things will be slow for a while.' I was referring to business.

"'There'll be opportunities out there. It's a matter of being in the right place at the right time.' We were skirting around the unspoken topic.

"Frankly, I was concerned that Simon was paying insufficient attention either to the boat or to the weather conditions. Maybe I was just the nervous type, but he was sailing almost into the eye of the wind, and the sail was starting to flap furiously. I expected the boat to go into irons any minute. He looked distracted, almost unstrung. And come to think of it, where were the jokes?

"'You've got the best analysts in the industry,' said Simon. 'And we have the investors, because we're out wooing them.' I had to admit that was a fair summary of our relative strengths.

"'You could put it another way. Your team is always out, and you're never at your desks,' I said, teasing him. 'We're there for our clients.' The truth was, Simon and I each had our niche. I related to the researchers and knew their language. They felt comfortable with me, and I with them. But the selling part of the job doesn't come easily in my case. I could never do what Simon does, out there working the politicos and the posh crowd."

"Yes," said Richard, pausing to take a drink from his water bottle. "You've either got it or you haven't. Selling's a talent."

Alan ran his fingers through his closely cropped hair and resumed his story.

"'We're moving into a new phase,' Simon told me. 'It may be short, but the people who get out and about will win the race. That's my strength, people. You know that. I also know my own weaknesses, though. Research, systems and back office.'

"The wind was rising in intensity, whipping the foam off the wave tops. I stared fixedly at the horizon, fighting back a rising nausea. I told myself I was not going to be seasick, not in front of Simon. Besides, we seemed to be getting somewhere. Simon clearly saw our respective skills as complementary. But I was beginning to get impatient. I thought I'd try to move things forward.

"'Are you looking to improve your office support?'

"'Look, Alan, you're the best in the business. You know that,' he said. Ah, flattery, meat and drink to the egotistical classes! 'It may not be a good time to change jobs. Last in, first out.

But if it's a question of working with someone like you, well, it might make sense.'

"'I understand that. I just wanted to know how you felt about your current team.'

"'We'll talk later,' Simon yelled, the wind blowing his words away.

"And then the boat heeled over as we cleared the Needles and emerged into the open Channel. The wind was gusting up to force seven and I had to brace myself against the side of the cockpit. A light rain began to add to the discomfort. As we crested each wave and sank into the next trough, salt spray streamed down my yellow wind-cheater. A siren shrieked in warning. Unseen by both of us, a coastal tanker, steaming westwards had crept up to leeward and passed only fifty feet away.

"'I'm taking her into Yarmouth,' Simon shouted. 'Stand by to go about . . . lee−o.' The sheets whipped and the sails thrashed furiously as we turned tail and scudded back to the relative shelter of the island.

"Yarmouth harbor was filled with small yachts avoiding the gale. We scouted about but couldn't find a mooring. So we dropped anchor near the harbor mouth. I was chilled. There was no way we could use the dinghy to get ashore in the wind and the rain, which was now beating down. We were holed up on board.

"'Come down and get warm,' Simon said as he headed for the cabin. I suspected that his idea of getting warm was another double scotch. There was no food aboard aside from some crisps. But at least we could shed our wind-cheaters and make ourselves comfortable.

"'Sorry about this. The wind's fighting the tide!'

"No sooner had he spoken than there was an ominous grinding sound. I felt the boat shudder as it collided with something. Simon shot from the cabin. A cascade of water fell through the hatchway.

"'Goddamn it!' Simon's urbane mask slipped. Our anchor had dragged, and we had drifted leeward onto an old, un-kempt, wooden boat moored downwind from us. The bowsprit of the boat was lodged precisely amidships, caught in our rig-ging. I leapt on deck, closing the hatch but forgetting my wet weather gear. It was still raining hard and the wind was blow-ing us onto the smaller vessel. I grabbed a boathook and tried to stop the intruding bowsprit from carrying away our stays. Simon joined me, wrestling with the bowsprit itself.

"'Bloody thing,' he yelled, 'just as well the owners aren't aboard. Keep pushing, goddamn it! We'll be in deep shit if we can't sort this one! Come forward, by me! I can't push off by myself, you idiot!'

"I joined Simon, pushing with all my strength. We put down fenders between the two hulls.

"'You don't see many boats like this around these days,' said Simon, gesturing at the older boat. 'No one's got the time or patience to keep them up. It shows, too. Look at that var-nish.'

"My head was pounding from the tension. The wind eased for a moment, the bowsprit came free. Hoping to secure us temporarily with a line to the smaller boat, Simon leapt onto its deck but fell awkwardly, crying out in pain. Limping around the deck, he was able to spring the painters so that the two boats rode together comfortably in the gale. I helped him back aboard and into the warm cabin. He had cut his knee and sprained his ankle, and he treated me to a stream of forthright language.

"'Where's the bloody first aid kit?' growled Simon.

"'Don't bloody ask me. How should I know?' I replied.

"'I told Caroline to put it back on board. Bloody women, never do what you ask them to do. Would you believe, she's invited people for dinner tonight. I told her it was a dodgy thing to do since I was going out on the boat. We had a bloody row about it.'

"It wasn't the sort of day Simon had planned. I found the first aid kit after all and bandaged the wound as best I could. Personally I had no plans for the evening, so I was all right. Besides, the liquor had put me into a mild stupor.

"'Pour yourself another scotch, old man. I'll put the heating on. I can just hear my wife lecturing me for not turning up at her bloody dinner party. Does your wife do that? Pick on you for every damn little thing? Caroline's totally preoccupied with her own life. We hardly speak to each other unless we're organizing some event. Not even in bed! By the time we get there, we're both too tired for, you know.'

"'Sex?' I laughed. 'That'll be the day!' I toweled my face and hair and put on dry clothes from the nearby locker. Simon was sprawled on the bunk, looking grim.

"'And you married to an actress! I was feeling envious. Must be some stud, I thought, with a wife like that.'

"'Envious of *me*?' I couldn't believe it. 'You, the Cambridge graduate with a perfect CV and a family to match?'

"'Looks good,' Simon said, 'but the reality is we've grown so far apart it's hard to remember what it was once like. That's what happens to two busy people, I suppose.'

"'Ever been tempted?'

"'Tempted? Shit, yes. But she'd cream me in a divorce court. My affairs have been with different brands of liquor.' Simon sank back on the bunk with a fresh double scotch, grimacing with pain.

"'You've got your kids,' I remarked, hoping to make him feel better.

"'Yeah, tell me about it! The older one, the budding novelist, is a raving pinko. Hates what I do and complains about financiers and globalization. We hardly speak. The middle one, well, she got in with the wrong crowd at college and . . . oh hell, what's the difference, who cares? I've had to send her for treatment. She moved on from speed to bloody heroin and I had to have her rescued from a seedy commune in Liverpool. Now you know. The younger one's going through the usual teenage rebellion. It's a bundle of fun.'

"'Any pictures?'

"Simon burrowed in a drawer and took out a fistful of photographs. The three girls were blonde and anorexic.

"'I guess it's our fault. We're never there for them,' he moaned.

"The cabin became warmer, insulated from the gale outside, snug and soporific. Our dumb companion was the bottle, and it silently did its work.

"'It'll blow itself out in an hour or two,' Simon said. 'Hope you weren't planning to work tonight.'

"'If I were, I now have an excuse.'

"'Would your conscience be clearer if you practiced some mergers and acquisitions? There's a Monopoly set on board.'

"So we settled into Monopoly, British version of course. I went for properties in the West End and he grabbed the utilities. Simon was not holding his drink well. From grumpy bad temper he turned silent and preoccupied, throwing the dice across the board so hard I had to scramble around on the cabin floor to retrieve them. His attention wandered and I was able to pick up a hotel before he realized he'd missed an opportunity. We started a second bottle of whisky."

"Sounds as if you found Simon in the middle of a midlife crisis," ventured Richard.

"Quite. Where was the bonhomie he was famous for? Simon was turning out to be more serious than I had expected him to be. And when he noticed I'd taken the hotel, he started going sentimental on me.

"'Know something?' he said. 'I used to wonder what it would be like to run a hotel in Mayfair. Come to that, to run any business. Start it, see it grow, know "I created this." Like a God, I tell other people how to manage their affairs and I even take a piece of the action if it looks really good. But I don't really know what it's like, running my own business.'

"'You wouldn't get out of merchant banking, would you?'

"'Hardly. It's like a drug, isn't it? Where else can you get a daily high and a million a year for doing what you enjoy?'

"'A million?' I suspected this was bravado. 'A bad year was it, last year?' A bit of sarcasm was irresistible, if imprudent. But he didn't seem to mind.

"'You know what I mean,' he slurred. 'What else would I do?'

"'I used to dream of becoming a country squire,' I said, 'with a manor house, a cloth cap, a shotgun and a dog. Making it into the leisured class, no more grubbing around for the rent. Well, I've got a big house now, but it's dark when I get home. I may as well be a lodger passing through. And if I had a dog, I'd barely have time to feed it. But I agree. Leave merchant banking? Wouldn't think of it. Incidentally, that's three houses on Park Lane, please.'

"'You get to a level of income and the idea of a normal wage frightens the shit out of you,' said Simon, paying no attention to the fact that I was taking him to the cleaners in Monopoly.

"'Your outfit's all right, though, isn't it?' I asked. 'I mean, despite the market?'

"Simon was silent. The wind was screaming through the rigging and the rain was drumming on the cabin roof. The two boats, lashed together, were yawing from side to side in the gale. Simon hobbled to the hatch to check that the fenders were in place. 'Bloody weather!' he said, as buckets of rainwater cascaded into the cabin. I noticed he had avoided answering my question.

"'I went into financial services because of my wife,' I said. 'Acting's an insecure way of life. We've never actually talked about it, but my income has allowed her to take the parts she really wanted, without doing commercials. Now she's successful and I hardly see her. She takes it for granted—the fancy clothes, the holidays, the choice of cars. People look aghast when I tell them I'm doing fifteen hour days at my age. But it's my own decision, at least in part. Frankly, it's like war. You live on adrenaline. Time and seasons pass by un-noticed.'

"'What about keeping the buzz but lowering the hours, having a bit more fun?'

"I thought, *Is he suggesting I join him? Being front man is not my forte, not really. Maybe I could drop my role as Chief Beggar and just concentrate on supervising the Nursemaids. God knows, this chap needs it.*

"But I said, 'Chance would be a fine thing!'

"'I'll be straight with you, Alan,' he told me. 'I got you down here because I thought you might need a little help on the deal-making side.'

"'You mean, if I joined your group I could concentrate on research and backup?'

"'Tell you the truth, old boy,' he sounded like a drunk from a thirties movie. 'I'm not talking about you joining me. I'm suggesting *I* join *you.*'

"For a moment I was speechless. *Should I laugh or cry?* 'So you admire the way I thrash you at Monopoly?' I quipped, stalling for time.

"'Screw the game,' Simon replied.

"'Do I understand you correctly?'

"'I've worked my arse off, made some huge bloody profits, and kept the place afloat while half the overseas staff were embezzling.' His voice dropped to a whisper. 'Already last quarter things started to soften up. Our revenues ramped up slower than expected. Management claimed that our earnings remained intact and our pipelines were building. But I knew better. Then we had that *huge* drop in the market. You remember the last time that happened? Masses of people laid off and not a chance of a new listing for months? Farewell to the companies we'd been nursing along. No more dinners, no more golf outings. Well, guess what? I've been talking exit strategies to one lot, discussing merger possibilities with another, and telling a third group to shove their dreams of an IPO! I'm peering up from a deep hole, my friend. Shall we drink to economic recovery?'

"We drank to it. And I got the picture. No revenues, no job. Not even for a golden boy like Simon. My sense of panic, almost nausea, peaked. Clearly there was no job offer forthcoming.

"'Tell me more about that delicious wife of yours,' he said. Cheeky bugger, playing games with me and now sticking pins in sensitive tissue. But I was beginning to warm to him. I realized I felt more comfortable with Simon, knowing he was going through hard times.

"So I replied: 'Last seen half-naked on a Cannes beach with a hunk from central casting, if you want the truth. I'm her excuse for extricating herself from lechers. Yes, that's what it's come down to.'

"'Well, your *kids* seem to value you. Let's drink to good old Dad!'

"We drank to good old Dad.

"'Which would you prefer if you were a kid?' I asked Simon, wallowing in my gloom. 'A sexy mom breaking into art films, or a stressed-out, graying old dad with ulcers?'

"'That's a choice?'

"'Anyway, they're into their friends, not their parents. They've been through one divorce, like most of the mates they drink with. Maybe that's enough.' I felt relaxed and drained my glass.

"'Well, they're alienated from the family, aren't they?' said Simon. 'And it's not surprising. Everyone is. *I'm* alienated from the family. It's a mess. I used to think I was damn near killing myself for the kids. Not really. I was doing it for me. To hell with Universal & Global Capital Incorporated. Life's too short.' With an expansive gesture he swept dice, cards, paper money, and plastic houses and hotels across the cabin. The Monopoly board was clear and uncluttered. We felt on the same wavelength.

"'To unemployment: yours—and mine!' I held out my glass for a toast.

"'You too? You sneaky bugger!'

"'Well, not officially. But the writing's on the wall. I'm forty five.'

"'Nobody loves a fairy when he's forty.' We sang this bit. 'And I was thinking, at least I know one guy out there who has his feet under the table.'

"And so, on that fateful day, we made a pact and sealed it with the remains of that second bottle of fifteen-year-old Macallan. We decided to start a small investment banking service together, looking for companies thinking ahead of the ball, and providing some investment advice on the side to small firms. Firms where we could build up a good personal rapport with management, unconstrained by the overhead of a multinational.

"Simon does the glad-handing; he's good at that. I run the show day-to-day. Simon's already left his wife. He's moved in with a pretty little homemaker who has vowed to get him off the wagon and have him looking forty again. Of course, we're working all the hours God gives."

"Why start a new company?" asked Richard. "With all the money you made, couldn't you just take a few nonexecutive directorships?"

"It's an obsession, I suppose. In any case, I *need* the money."

Randall turned this last remark over slowly in his head. "How did you get home that day?"

"Both boats drifted onto a mudbank on a falling tide, and we had to wait four hours for the tide to refloat us. But we got off all right, nobody irreparably hurt. A metaphor, I suppose."

"So you didn't actually get, you know. . . ."

"Sacked? Well, yes, I did. The notice they give you is in direct proportion to your time with the company. I'd been there ten years, so they gave me ten minutes to clear my desk."

"Dreadful, the way some of these firms treat their staff," said Richard. "But at least you're in better shape now, navigating your own ship, as it were."

Alan halted and stared at the view for a moment, his jaw tense. "I hope like hell you're right," he replied. His companions looked at him expectantly.

"The day before I left home for this trip," he continued, "I went into the office to do some last minute chores. While I was there the phone rang. A man's voice on the other end of the line asked for Simon. I explained that Simon was out of the office. Who was speaking? He wouldn't give me his name, just gave me a phone number and left a message for Simon to call him. But I recognized the voice. It was Sean Parsons, the CEO of Universal & Global Capital, Simon's old firm. I had met him on several occasions, had heard him speak at banking functions."

"Why would he want to speak to Simon?" asked Randall.

"Good question! Unless. . . . The fact is, business has picked up and everyone in the business knows that Universal & Global Capital are hiring again."

"Oh, hell!" said Richard. A sense of alarm hung in the breeze.

"We've only been in business a matter of months," said Alan. "When we started, we didn't really know one another. But things were going well, and I thought, *What's the point in having your own show if you can't have a break for a week or so?* So I booked this walk to Rome. Now, I don't know whether I'll have a business to go back to. And I can't raise Simon on the phone."

Alan's cellphone rang. His hand fumbled furiously with the instrument hanging on his belt. The three men stopped and moved to the side of the farm road they were headed up, letting the other walkers pass them by.

"Excuse me a minute. Yes, yes. Don't worry. The market's a bit soft, but we'll see it through. Trust me. Have you got those figures? Great! E-mail them, will you? Where am I? Oh, in a field somewhere in France. No problem, I'm on a satellite link. Just send as normal. . . ."

There was a moment of silence.

"Simon could just be busy. Or maybe his cellphone's out of order." Randall, cool and imperturbable, was doing his best to calm his companion.

"I've already left three messages for him," replied Alan, shaking his head. "You know, I really feel uneasy. I'm not going to be able to enjoy this trip."

"Give it another day or two," said Randall. "You're here now."

"I can't do it. Talking to you two has helped, but . . . I need to get back to the office," said Alan. "How the hell do I get to Charles de Gaulle from here?"

"It's probably quicker to return to Calais and take the ferry," said Richard and started to add, *If you walked across the Channel last time, maybe this time you could flap your arms around a bit and fly.* But he glanced at Alan and thought better of it.

The Lawyer's Tale

Nigel

One must not mock the lawyer; he's the grease,
The nexus separating grief and peace.
This lawyer's squat and heavy, with a stoop,
The natural intermediary of the group.
Where tiredness, irritation cause offense,
He scurries, sweat on brow, to calm the tense.
Enjoying gossip, he, with darting eyes,
Unravels that which subtly underlies
The spoken word. His analytic mind
Conceals a nature these days hard to find.
His sole concern is not *res judicata,*
He can enjoy a painting or sonata.
Oft in the Inns of Court will he make glisten
The eyes of hardened jurists as they listen.
Oh! This model lawyer, happy sample!
Would there were others following his example!

With the beautiful cathedral of Laon in our minds, its perfect proportions in stark contrast to our lives, we proceeded to Aubigny au Laonnais and walked steadily downhill, only to climb up again to a tall forest that opened onto a large Roman fort. It was circular in shape and dated back to the days when Caesar began his Gallic campaign. Elderflower bushes surrounded us as we climbed a hill above the fort and sat down with a splendid view across fields of wheat and sugar beets.

A group gathered around Nigel, the lawyer, who was squinting into the distance, his black bushy eyebrows contrasting with his pallid face. Unfit at this stage of the trip, he would typically pant up the slopes and then pause to recover, wiping his glistening forehead.

"Have you noticed the big, open fields belonging to that estate?" asked Nigel. "They're unusual for France. French farms tend to be small and uneconomical, I think partly because of the inheritance laws. I'm not sure."

"I'm told that if you're a foreigner and you die owning a French farm it can be a dreadful hassle," commented Gerald, the retired colonel.

"It can indeed. I tell my clients with property here to find a good French lawyer. Don't talk to me."

"Is that your line of work, wills and estates?"

"I'm a solicitor," said Nigel. "I handle a variety of legal work, but probate is an important part of my business. The little chateau you see over there reminds me of an interesting case I had. Here, let's sit down. I'll tell you the story while you enjoy the view. You can draw the moral yourselves.

"I was friendly at university with a chap called Michael. One day he came to me in a terrible state, wanting my help on an inheritance issue. Michael's great-grandfather had made a fortune from shipping in the late nineteenth century and had equipped himself with a title and a country estate in the most desirable part of County Durham. In due course, his grandson and Michael's father, Lord Ackley, inherited this family property along with substantial financial assets.

"The property included a seventeenth-century manor house with a very fine carved wood staircase. It had fallen into disuse until Michael's great-grandfather restored it. No farmland remained attached to the house, but there was a long grass terrace bordered by flowers and shrubs. The terrace led to a walled garden enclosing an orchard with old varieties of fruit trees and a large patch of berry bushes. I saw the place once. It was lovely and well maintained. In time, Lord Ackley added central heating, and also a pool and tennis court. He lived there as a comfortable country squire on the income from his inheritance."

"Nice life," said Darryl, the personal trainer, picking at a bag full of mixed nuts and dried fruit.

"When Michael was just fourteen and his sister Sarah was twelve, Lord Ackley developed a rare and fatal disease. As he was relatively young at the time, he hadn't prepared a will. But on his deathbed he did in fact dictate and sign a will, leaving about a quarter of his financial assets to his two children and the remainder of his estate, including the house and gardens, to his wife, Jessica, so she could stay there and raise the children. His minister and doctor were witnesses to the will.

"There was a problem, however. Lord Ackley's will was inconsistent with the terms of the estate he had inherited. Whether this was deliberate or due to his failing health is not known. He was barely alive at the time, and there was also an issue as to whether those around him exerted undue influence. Now this gets a bit complicated, so let me know if I lose you."

"I'm with you so far," said Gerald.

"Well, Lord Ackley's grandfather had left his money as well as the house and gardens in an estate 'in fee tail male,' meaning it was limited to male descendants. This kind of estate can be distinguished from the more common 'estate in fee simple,' which places no restrictions on the beneficiary. 'Entailing,' or restricting, an estate was more common in the nineteenth century, and it applied only to land. It was a way of keeping estates together.

"Later, a major change to the law of property allowed you to include cash and investments as long as it was done through a trust. So Lord Ackley's grandfather put his entire real and personal property into a trust for his male descendants. The girls were expected, as you probably know, to marry into their own estates in those days, although not all did.

"So here comes the problem. The trustee was Lord Ackley's father's bank manager. He had known the family for years. The children were still young and their mother, Jessica, had no other means of support. So he decided to use Lord Ackley's will as grounds to 'disentail' the estate—that is, to remove the restriction to male descendants—and convert it into an 'estate in fee simple.' The court found this plan to be in the spirit of more recent legislation allowing for commonsense interpretation of estates and trusts, and the entailment was barred, that is, ended. After all, this was implicit in Lord Ackley's will. The trustee thought Lord Ackley had settled a reasonable sum on the children, including the male heir Michael, and Jessica would presumably leave the children the remainder of the estate when she died."

"Must have been hard on the children, to lose a father at that age," said Moira, resting against her backpack. As a counselor, Moira was more interested in human relationships than in the finer points of British law.

"Michael never talked about it much," continued Nigel. "He was always a bit of a loner, and tried not to let his feelings show. But at boarding school he had a friend called Richard. I had also known Richard at university, although he was not, like Michael, on my staircase in college, so I didn't know him well. He was the son of a vicar, and by all reports a determined young man. He made the rugger and cricket teams at school by persistence as much as by talent. And he was a good student, better than Michael.

"Richard was supportive of Michael during the period following his father's death, and the two apparently became inseparable. I think they complemented each other in a fundamental way, although neither was particularly outgoing. Michael was shy but full of energy. He had a lot of ideas, even if some of them were half-baked. Richard was less imaginative but more thoughtful. He possessed a quiet charm. The two confided in each other and spent their holidays together, mainly at Michael's house or at the beach with Michael's mother and sister. Richard's parents had little money and were preoccupied with their parish.

"As they grew older, Richard fell in love with Sarah, Michael's sister. Michael told me that he'd hoped the two would someday marry. But Sarah went off to university and apparently fell for a good looking young man with family money and political ambitions. Shortly after graduating, Sarah married him. Richard was dismayed. This was his first real setback. But Michael stuck by him, tried to cheer him up. In any case, he found Sarah's husband brash and pushy and didn't much like him. So Richard and Michael remained friends.

"Now, as I understand it, Richard had arranged to meet Michael at his house one afternoon but arrived while Michael was still out. Michael heard what happened later. His mother, Jessica, was on the tennis court practicing her serve. She was a bit of a flirt and, still in her mid-forties, very attractive.

"'Game of tennis, Richard?' she asked.

"'I don't have my shoes,' Richard replied.

"'Borrow Michael's,' she said.

"Well, from such small accidents of fate, great affairs are born. Before the year was out Richard married Jessica, making him Michael's stepfather.

"Michael had a good sense of humor, but he wasn't sure how funny this particular development was. He agreed to give his mother away, but refused to give the best man's speech at the reception, arguing that it didn't make sense for him to do both at the same wedding. 'It's a bit much,' he remarked to me. 'My best friend and my mother!'"

"Can't blame the chap," said Gerald, looking up from a copy of the *Daily Telegraph* that he had brought with him.

"In due course, Michael met and married Jane, a vivacious young teacher in a school for gifted children in West Hartlepool. They had a daughter, Emma, early in their marriage, and she remained an only child despite Jane's efforts to have more children. Michael used his inheritance to set himself up as a shipping broker, but he didn't have the confidence or the personality to attract big contracts. He spent as much as he earned on the business and had to draw heavily on his inheritance, which dwindled and eventually ran out. He and Jane occasionally saw Richard and Jessica socially, but Michael felt awkward around them.

"Michael had always had the gadgets, the better clothes and the nicer home. Now the tables were turned. Richard, the relatively poor son of a vicar, was living in Michael's family house, eating fruit out of Michael's family orchard, playing croquet on Michael's family lawn, and gazing over the pond where, at age six, Michael had turned the water bright red with a bottle of poster color. Michael told me he would think of the irony of this situation as he drove up the driveway.

"I don't think at this point Michael was an envious man. His real anxiety was his own lack of business acumen. If his grandfather could make a fortune it ought to be in his blood as well. And so he attended birthday and Christmas celebrations at the manor house and pretended to Richard that his business was successful. But he waited a long time before returning invitations.

"After ten years or so, Jessica developed breast cancer. It spread before it was detected. She put up a good fight, but it was not long before the disease took over and Jessica died. Jessica's will stated that if her husband died first, her estate would be divided equally between her two children. But if she died first, which she did, the majority of the estate would go to Richard, allowing him to stay in the manor house where they had been so happy together. The remainder of her financial assets would be put in trust for her grandchildren. So Richard, Michael's best friend, now became Jessica's main beneficiary and the sole owner of the family home. Michael and his sister Sarah received nothing.

"Several years prior to Jessica's death, Sarah had given up on her philandering husband and asked for a divorce. I remember meeting Sarah once at a dinner party. 'He can't see a good-looking woman without testing out his mating call,' she told me after a few drinks. I suppose she confided in me knowing that I had been friendly with Michael. The court awarded her a sizeable alimony and a modest lump sum. When Jessica became ill, Sarah was there to help Richard care for her and arrange the funeral.

"At first Richard was in a state of shock, and I think Sarah was still feeling too hurt and alienated by her divorce to think about a new relationship. But in the months following Jessica's death, Sarah visited Richard frequently and they comforted each other over lunch or afternoon tea on the grassy terrace. Then one day Richard invited Sarah for a candlelit supper and a year later Michael's stepfather became his brother-in-law."

"So Richard got the girl after all!" said Moira, always pleased at a happy outcome.

"Yes, although it may have been she who caught the fish. I met Sarah only that once, but she struck me as strong-willed. In any case, once married, it seems she missed the social life she had led in London with her upwardly mobile husband. So she went to London once a week to shop for clothes or see some old friends. And she became an active hostess and participant in community affairs in County Durham.

"Richard followed her lead, supporting local charitable events and lunching with business and civic leaders. He became interested in wine and developed a cellar that was the envy of the local gentry. He designed his own in the bowels of the old manor house and then supervised the lighting, the fitting of racks, and the purchase of fine wines from around the world. Having started this hobby in midlife, he stuck to the classics. Richard was generous with his wine and liked to surprise and please his guests by uncorking an old Barolo or a first-growth Bordeaux.

"While Richard blithely continued his fortuitous life as the squire of squires, I found Michael growing more dispirited. Here he was, working week in, week out, scraping a living, while Richard lived as if to the manor born. Acceptance changed slowly and subtly into feelings of frustration and even exasperation, as he was reminded repeatedly of the reversal of fortunes—the poor now comfortable, the rich reduced. Was it, he asked me over a beer in a pub one day, just life? Or was it unjust life?

"Now, history has a way of repeating itself. One rainy November night, about ten years after she married Richard, Sarah died returning home from London. Richard took a call from the policeman. 'It's about your wife, sir. I'm afraid there's been an accident.' Sarah was killed on the A1(M), not far from Northallerton."

Nigel paused as the sun disappeared behind the scudding clouds, and the temperature fell.

"Richard was devastated. He had apparently hoped for children. Sarah had not been interested, and now she was dead. But Sarah had been grateful to Richard for his love and support and had made him her sole beneficiary. Her inheritance from her father, initially the size of Michael's, had been invested well over the years and was virtually intact. So Richard received a sizeable portfolio of stocks and bonds. Michael, her brother, received nothing from her estate.

"At this point, I'm sure that Michael felt a rising tide of resentment. Richard, the sole heir of his mother, had now become the sole heir of his sister. He, next of kin, received nothing, a ghost at the banquet. To make matters worse, he had, as he once wryly joked, missed the boat on containerization. He was left trying to broker coastal shipping destined for the Scandinavian countries. Bits and pieces, wherever he could find cargo and free space. He had tried a variety of marketing angles and traveled frequently to search for new clients, but profits were stagnant. Jane had continued to work, but the truth was that he and Jane were having difficulty making ends meet. They lived in a small house on a busy street and Jane shopped for food and clothing in the least expensive shops.

"Jane didn't share Michael's feelings of resentment. She had never had more than a modest income and there was no question of her being heir to Jessica's and Sarah's fortunes. She had a generous nature and invited Richard, who was now twice widowed, to drop by the house any time he was feeling lonely. After all, Richard was Emma's godfather and perhaps he could knock some sense into her. Neither she nor Michael could.

"Emma was nineteen and a weak candidate for university. She had no strong interests, either professional or romantic. She lolled around the house, bored and ill-tempered. Meanwhile, Michael's frequent travels meant he was seldom at home and, when he was, he was tired and preoccupied. Although kind at heart, Michael was an introvert, not well-suited to modern fatherhood. He had had a correct but distant relationship with his parents, who seldom visited him at school. Had he thought about it at all, Michael might have concluded that getting too close to a child was not good for discipline or mutual respect. I'm sure he was not intentionally unavailable, it was just that he did not know how else to behave. Jane had done what she could and thought Richard might give Emma the strong hand she needed.

"In the following months, Richard became the father-friend that Emma never had, taking her to the races, fancy restaurants, and museums in London. Only he wasn't her father. Richard was rich, well dressed and reasonably attractive, a man of the world who told amusing stories. He treated her as an adult, as an equal. The truth was, Emma was at a loose end. For his part, Richard felt sorry for the girl, and he wanted some companionship.

"Michael later told me about a conversation with his wife around this time. He knew his wife was less suspicious than he was and also less worried about money, but he had a recurring thought that was beginning to haunt him.

"'Do you think Richard is after the money?' he asked.

"'You mean the money your mother left in trust for the grandchildren?'

"'As the only grandchild, Emma will be a rich woman in two years time. I was hoping she might invest in the business. After all, it's family money.'

"'It's her life and her money,' said Jane.

"Within six months Richard proposed to Emma and she accepted. Richard was now to become Michael's son-in-law and the potential heir to Emma's fortune. Emma was unlikely to ever ask her father's advice on investments and equally unlikely to ever think of investing in his business on her own.

"It was at this point that Michael came to see me formally at my office near the Inns of Court. He looked as if he hadn't slept for weeks. His jaw was set and his words sounded bitter. He explained to me that Richard had been the sole heir to his mother and his sister and now he was engaged to marry his daughter and would have substantial influence, to say the least, over the last of the family money.

"'It's not only unjust, it's intolerable,' he said. 'That damn fellow seems to be deliberately sucking me dry—my family money, my self-confidence, my sanity! What can I do?'

"I inquired as to what options he had already considered. Michael said he had thought of asking Richard to share some of his money, but Richard would have presumably done this already if he were so inclined. He also thought of asking Richard to invest in his business, but Richard was no fool and would have wanted to see the accounts. Finally he thought of suing Richard, but as far as he knew the wills were clear and there were no grounds for a suit.

"Or were there?

"I felt sympathy for Michael and, for a fee, offered to review the wills to see if there were any irregularities on which to base a legal case for claiming some of the money. I assigned a conscientious young articled clerk to the case.

"It quickly became apparent that Michael might have a good chance to recover some, if not all, of his father's estate by suing the trustee who had disentailed it. One could make the case that none of Michael's female relations should have benefited from his family's estates—not Jessica, not Sarah, not Emma. And thus they would have had nothing to leave to Richard. The entire estate should have passed on to Michael.

"I hated being in the middle of this. When I contacted Richard with the news that Michael could be (subject to Court ruling) the rightful owner of all he had inherited from Jessica and Sarah, and that Emma's trust would likely also revert to Michael, Richard sat down with a stiff drink. Or so he told me later.

"'What's got into him?' he asked me over the phone. He knew I had kept up with Michael over the years. 'If he needed money, why didn't he ask? I understand that he might be envious that the family estate was left to me and not to him. But this is preposterous!'

"If Michael won a law suit, Richard would be left with nothing. So, fearing that Michael was going to take him to court, Richard drove down to London and instructed his solicitor to explore all possible angles that might call Michael's suit into question. He told him to spare no expense. The two of them then consulted a Queen's Counsel in his chambers at Gray's Inn."

"Queen's Counsel? What's the difference between a Queen's Counsel and a solicitor?" asked Evelyn.

"A QC is a senior advocate, or trial lawyer, who has done his time in court and is well regarded. A solicitor, like myself, is a lawyer who handles matters out of court. In any event, Richard and his solicitor briefed the QC and were advised on the legal options.

"Six weeks later Richard received a call and again came down to London. His solicitor presented him with startling news.

"'It seems that Michael's father met his mother while working as a District Officer in Kenya during the war. They had a passionate affair and Jessica became pregnant. Michael's father was young and not ready to marry, but Jessica wanted to keep the baby and Michael was born out of wedlock. They eventually did marry and Sarah was also born in Kenya two years later. When they returned to England, they altered the date of their marriage."

"What a morass! No wonder you lawyers are paid so much!" said Gerald.

"At this point, it was 'checkmate.' On one side, Michael believed that he was the rightful heir to his father's entailed estate and that the trustee's action to disentail the estate was illegal. On the other side, Richard, on the advice of the QC, believed his inheritances would be upheld, given Michael's bastard status.

"But Michael had an ace up his sleeve. He pointed out that his father's deathbed signature was only a scratch and it might be possible to declare his will null and void. If Michael's father died intestate, Michael could claim at least partial rights to the estate under legislation passed in the late 1960s to enable an illegitimate child to succeed on the intestacy of his parents.

"As a solicitor, my approach was to advise Michael to arrive at a financial settlement with Richard out of court. Through mediation or arbitration, if necessary. This is normally what happens in inheritance disputes, and it certainly would have made sense in this case. But the stakes were too high and the tensions between the two men were too strong.

"Michael insisted on going to court. 'I have little to lose now,' he told me. 'Richard, on the other hand, has everything to lose.'

"This was all too thick for my blood from the start. However, I duly presented my 'Instructions to Counsel' on Michael's case to a barrister I knew at Lincoln's Inn. The barrister brought Michael's suit against the trustee to the Chancery Division of the High Court of Justice. Remember, the trustee had disentailed Lord Ackley's estate shortly after his death, on the grounds that it was Lord Ackley's wish, as implied in his will, to bar the entail male.

"The day of the trial arrived. The judge held that, although Lord Ackley's signature was valid and he did not die intestate, the trustee had insufficient grounds for disentailment and Lord Ackley's bequests to Sarah and Jessica, and hence to Emma, conflicted with the original restriction, 'in tail male,' placed on the estate by his grandfather. He also ruled that Michael's claim to the estate—and, for that matter, Lord Ackley's original bequest to him—was incompatible with the original restriction, as Michael's great grandfather had specified that the male descendant be born in wedlock.

"The upshot of this unusual case was that neither Michael nor Richard was the 'heir in tail' to the original estate. Michael received nothing and Richard had to move out of the manor house and give up most of his financial portfolio. The court took over these assets and contacted the rightful heir, rumored to be a prominent lawyer living in Australia."

We all sat in silence as we pondered the mesh of emotions provoked by wills.

"What happened to Michael?" Shirley, the bureaucrat, had been following every detail of the complicated case with increasing interest.

"Well, to his credit, Michael laughed when he heard the verdict. He laughed until tears ran down his cheeks. I suppose it *was* rather funny.

"The last I heard, Richard had moved into a tiny cottage in the Cotswolds and Emma had left him for a younger man she'd known at school. Richard went to visit Michael and Jane, bringing a cheap bottle of wine. They drove up the hill facing the old family manor house and had a picnic on the grass. Michael recounted to me their conversation.

"'Remember old Philip Grantley, used to thrash us as we leapt into the cold bath at school at seven in the morning?' Michael asked.

"And Richard replied, 'Yeah, he was a bloody pervert!'

"The two men apparently sat there, gazing at the manor house, which had been a home for both of them.

"'Hey, look!' said Richard. 'Do you see what that sonofabitch has done? He's taken down the greenhouse! I had prize orchids in there!'

"'It's one thing to lose it all, but to a bloody lawyer!'"

- The Airline Pilot's Tale -

Randall

An airline pilot, chisel-featured, cool,
Who's been a heartthrob since he was at school,
Stands firm, with not a sculpted hair displaced,
A Florentine museum he could grace.
With darkened glasses, gently shifting hips,
A sensual smile, amused, plays on his lips.
A man of few words, with calm and steady eye,
To questions gives a reticent reply,
Deflecting probing queries on his life
(Why is he alone, is there a wife?)
With comments on the weather or the view,
Adroitly focusing the talk on you.
The women think him gorgeous, neat and trim;
The men, more cautious, feel unsure of him.
And well they might, for it is still unclear
Whose heart he'll conquer, simply standing there.

Following an old Roman road, we walked through a forest and then out across the closely planted vineyards. The sun beat down, and we watched in dismay as the crop dusters flew by overhead. Part way down the slope, a table awaited us, crowded with coolers and tasting glasses supplied by the local wine society. Ah, champagne! The short introduction seemed an eternity to our thirsty crew. The smaller the bubble, the finer the taste. Did we care?

Starting with a "Blanc de Blanc," we moved up the scale to the *pinots noirs* and then to the *pinots chardonnais*, the non vintage and the vintage. Sipping slowly, we smiled and chatted. And Lizzie, the divorcée, and Nicola shared their recurring sexual fantasies about Randall.

The trip was well under way and neither woman had been able to attract the airline pilot's attention. Together they observed a slightly tipsy Randall, who was happily gazing down on Epernay and wondering perhaps if his next holiday might bring him back this way again. They decided on a joint approach.

"Let's have your story, Randall," said Nicola, going for a direct overture. "We're not letting you off the hook!"

"You may wonder why I'm *walking* to Rome, but you see very little up there at thirty-six-thousand feet," said Randall. "Just cloud. Then, you come back to earth and find yourself in some faceless hotel that looks like the same faceless hotel you stayed in at the last stop. Anyway, it's good to travel on land for a change. I was never much for a busman's holiday."

"Don't you like being a pilot?" asked Lizzie, unconsciously primping her blonde bouffant hair.

"Oh, I wouldn't say that. It's well paid, and it's what I know. Actually, I'm pretty much out of the business now. Just enough to keep up my license."

"How did you get into flying in the first place?" asked Nicola, who liked to take things from the beginning.

"I was a pilot in Vietnam, flying off carriers. I'd always wanted to be a flier, and it never occurred to me to avoid the draft. My father served in the Marine Air Corps during World War II. Got shot down and was locked up on the ground floor of an Austrian whorehouse. His sleeping quarters were right under a lady called 'Bedspring Helga.' He says that's how he developed the ability to sleep through anything."

Lizzie and Nicola exchanged wide-eyed glances. They both had an image of Randall as a gentleman, polite and reserved. That was the impression he gave.

"After 'Nam I flew company jets. I worked for GM, then IBM. Not a bad life. The corporate executive types knew how to travel in the seventies. Brooks Brothers suits, real leather luggage. They'd arrange for a flight over lunch or dinner, to save time, and start off with martinis and smoked salmon. You're always on call and you never know where you'll be headed next, but you get a fair amount of down time. Fortunately, I inherited my father's ability to sleep anywhere, anytime. It's a skill that comes in handy. Anyway, after a while I switched to commercial airlines. Just for a change, really. I started out international."

"Sounds romantic! Off to see the pyramids? Tahiti?" offered Lizzie.

"Romantic for a while, but I soon switched to a domestic airline. Fewer long hauls. But Reagan and the Republicans messed up the industry with deregulation, then wrecked the unions."

"It must be a lonely life for your wife," Nicola speculated with a wink to Lizzie.

"I'm not married."

"I guess there are just too many pretty stewardesses."

"Actually, stewardesses are now called flight attendants," said Randall, pretending not to have understood the drift of the conversation.

"Interesting distinction, if you think about it. 'Stewarding' implies looking after the passengers, trying to prevent them from drinking too much. 'Attending' implies passivity, just being there, waiting for a passenger to puke on the seats."

"Come on, Randall," said Nicola, with a flirtatious smile Lizzie hadn't seen before. "You're avoiding the question. Everyone knows that pilots have their pick of flight attendants."

Randall smiled. "In the old days you were often able to fly with the same people and get to know them. Pilots married stewardesses like bandleaders used to marry their singers. Now pilots are bus drivers. Often they don't see the same crew twice, the airlines have grown so big. But you say you're interested in pilots and flight attendants?"

"That's right," said Lizzie, with an encouraging tone, as they sat down on the side of the road within easy reach of the tasting table.

"Well, it reminds me of a story, a true story. Some twenty years ago I had a friend called Ralph, who was extremely handsome."

"Not unusual for a pilot," said Lizzie coyly.

"Ralph worked on standby for the same airline I did. He was one of our best pilots and didn't mind being called night or day. He was single, had no ties, and could nod off easily and sleep through anything. Standby pays a premium, so he made more than the average pilot. And all the female flight attendants had a crush on him, even the married ones. Their fondest dream was to get on a flight with Ralph.

"After a few years Ralph got fed up with standby and asked the company for a regular route. 'I'd like to see what you can come up with,' he said.

"Well, the company wasn't about to lose Ralph. Not only was he a first rate pilot and a professional, but he had a calm, reassuring manner, much commented on by passengers and crew alike."

"Empathy and confidence are important in any job," commented Nicola. "I know it is in mine."

"Well, the company offered Ralph two choices: San Francisco–Chicago–Dallas–San Francisco with two nights in the Bay area, or New York–Miami–Key West–Miami–New York with two nights in the Keys. The Keys route required switching from a standard jet to a small jet in Miami, since the traffic to Key West was relatively light, but management thought the extension to the Keys might be attractive. Or, Ralph could suggest his own route. But he took the Keys."

The young man from the wine society was making his rounds, bottle in hand. Nicola, Lizzie and Randall were holding out their glasses when a crop duster reappeared over the hill spraying the vines, the drinkers, and the half-filled champagne glasses. Randall, ever cool, scarcely paused.

"Ralph needed three flight attendants on the New York-Miami run, but only one on the smaller plane to Key West. The company had a rotation plan for attendants, and he knew he had to accept whoever was assigned to the Miami flight. There wasn't much he could do about that. But he might be able to choose which of the three would continue on to Key West. So he decided to take the Human Resources Director—we called him the HRD for short—for a beer.

"'Do me a favor, will you?' asked Ralph. 'Let me know who's assigned to the Miami flight. I'd like to have some input into who continues on to the Key West leg.'

"'I bet you would!' said the HRD. 'And so would I if I were in your place. Sure, I'll let you know. No problem.' And he laughed.

"Several weeks later, Ralph got a call from the HRD.

"'You know, you're a lucky s.o.b.,' he said. 'Meet me after work and I'll fill you in.' And he did.

"'Your first lucky break is that you didn't get a man. There are a lot of male attendants these days and your chances of getting three women are not as high as they used to be. But you did. They're all based in New York, so I know a little about each one. I suspect you've met a couple of them, if not all three.

"'Do you know Cheryl? The blonde, with tits out to here?' He holds his hand a foot in front of his chest. She's mid-thirties and very much married, but you'd never know it. The woman's got a terrific sense of humor and a store of jokes you wouldn't believe. Something that eludes most women.

"'Then there's Felicia. Not a bad choice either. She's the pert little brunette with all the energy. You've probably seen her around. Good natured, competent on the job, and patient with bad-tempered passengers. She's single, never been married, as far as I know. Seems rather sensitive.

"'The third girl assigned to the Miami flight is Amy. Not bad looking, and she's the intellectual of the group. Amy has a college degree from a good school, and she's smart, even if she does talk a lot. She's good at chatting up businessmen, and we've used her as a substitute in first class since she knows what the stock market's doing and reads the *Wall Street Journal*. She might be interesting to talk to if the occasion arose. But it's up to you. Really, Ralph, you've got some good choices here. Let me know what you decide.'

"Well, Ralph turned the question over in his mind for several days. Clearly discretion would be essential for the woman accompanying him to Key West. It might seem odd to someone outside the industry, but you have to remember we were a pretty tight family in those days, and news traveled fast. Ralph intended to have a good time on his rest stops and he didn't want to travel with someone unable to keep her mouth shut. He remembered his friend Pete, a pilot at IBM. Pete used to sleep with the secretaries on company trips, until rumors started going around that his performance in bed left something to be desired. Clearly, one of his traveling companions had been telling stories out of school. So discretion topped Ralph's list of desirable attributes for the girl on the Key West extension trip. But how to test it?

"He hit on an idea one morning on his way to work. That day, over coffee with Cheryl, he casually mentioned that the sales manager for the northeast was apparently having a torrid affair with Jennifer, the redheaded New Zealander.

"'Knowing Jennifer it seems unlikely, and the sales manager is due to retire. So I don't know if there's any truth in it. Anyway, don't tell anyone,' he said. 'It would be embarrassing for them if this sort of thing got around.'

"The next day Ralph arranged to have lunch with Amy and asked her if there was any truth in the rumor about Anna. Anna was the flight attendant with the longest service in the company and was slated for promotion to a high paid job in the CEO's office. The company gossip, he said, was that Anna was the best lay around. What had she been up to?

"'Look,' said Ralph. 'Maybe this is all above board. Please don't spread anything around. There could be nothing to it.'

"Lastly, he had a drink with Felicia. Was it true that Doug, one of the other pilots, was leaving his wife for a Ukrainian immigrant with long, dark hair and even longer legs?

"'I don't believe it, but I wondered if you'd heard anything,' said Ralph. 'Don't mention it to anyone. It would be embarrassing for all of them if it were untrue.' And having planted the seeds, he sat back and waited.

"Ralph wasn't fond of spreading rumors about colleagues. . . ."

"I'd hope not! It's not a very kind thing to do." Nicola frowned.

"But Ralph felt the stakes were high," continued Randall, a bit disconcerted at Nicola's remark. "His position of respect and his future in the company could be at stake at the hands of a gossip. You can understand that.

"Anyway, the scheme worked as expected. Within several days the rumor about Jennifer and the sales manager trickled back to him, and the following week two guys asked him if he had slept with Anna. Three weeks passed and he arranged for another beer with the HRD.

"'Tell me, have you heard anything about my friend Doug? Isn't he having marital problems?'

"'Not that I've heard,' said the HRD, 'and you know I keep tabs on that sort of thing. It's my job to know what's going on, even if it's off hours.'

"'Glad to hear it,' said Ralph. 'By the way, I'd like to take Felicia on the plane to Key West.'

"'Good choice,' said the HRD, with a knowing grin. 'I'd have picked her myself. Lucky fellow. Be gentle with her now.' Ralph gave him an enigmatic smile.

"Shortly thereafter personnel announced Ralph's new route. He'd be accompanied by Cheryl, Amy, and Felicia on the New York–Miami trip and by Felicia alone on the Key West leg. The two single women were old enough to know that the pool of potential partners diminishes with age. And I suspect Cheryl was also privately thrilled at this assignment, knowing there would be a line of flight attendants around the block to take her place if she dropped out—even if it didn't include the glamorous leg to the Keys.

"Felicia, of course, was delighted. She had retained her youth and innocence on the outside, but she was desperately lonely. I actually knew Felicia personally, as well as Ralph, and I once talked to her about this period of her life. She was nearing thirty and looking to settle down. She knew she was attractive to men, and she had had a series of relationships. But they never seemed to lead anywhere. Part of the problem was her job. Boyfriends seemed to dislike the suddenly empty calendar and moved rapidly to fill it, usually with another attractive woman. When she did find someone less impatient, she seemed to grow quickly critical of his character or his habits. Most of her boyfriends had been Latino, like herself, and she felt they expected her to put up with a lot. Her one big romance had been with a WASP, like Ralph. She had been deeply in love, but after six months or so he had dropped her with no explanation.

"I know that Felicia wanted a husband and kids, and she found Ralph attractive. She made no secret of the fact. Although ignorant of the conversations between Ralph and the HRD, she may have suspected that sometimes assignments are influenced by a pilot's preference. She had been with the company long enough to know that there were rules and there were rules. Some were there to be bent, if not broken. She probably wondered if Ralph had used his influence to work the system. And if so, why had he chosen her for the Key West extension? Felicia saw Ralph as a guy who held his cards close to his chest. I think she thought she could get him to loosen up and thought he sensed this as well. What better way to find out than two days a week in the Keys? But then, a man as good looking as Ralph was sure to have somebody around, wasn't he?

"As the target date for the new schedule approached, Felicia sharpened her assets. She went shopping for a more classic look. He might be looking for a woman who could fit in with business executives and professionals, not just technicians or low level service industry employees—the immigrant community she frequented. I suspect she was dreaming of a house in the suburbs, a wide lawn mowed by a neighborhood teenager, and a weekly barbecue for friends.

"I heard from a mutual friend that Felicia had a cut and blowdry, followed by a manicure and pedicure the day before departure. She bought copies of *Fortune* and *Esquire* and read them at home in the evening. Ralph seemed like a smart guy, and if she had time alone with him she wanted to connect with his mind as well as his body.

"So Ralph set off on his new route with three happy flight attendants. Felicia felt heady and full of anticipation. The other two cabin attendants were convinced they would fill in for Felicia at some point down the road and looked forward to that. So once they arrived in Miami, Amy and Cheryl waved a cheery goodbye to Ralph and Felicia, who rushed to board their connecting flight.

"Felicia's face was flushed with excitement as the small plane arrived in Key West. She had never been to the Keys before and imagined herself snorkeling among the reefs with Ralph. Opening the door, she felt the warm Florida air stirred by an evening sea breeze. She touched Ralph's hand as they stood waiting for the last passenger to deplane. Together they entered the small airport lounge.

"There, to greet them, was a slight young man with movie-star looks.

"'Tom!' said Ralph, his face more animated than Felicia had seen it. 'Good to see you. Felicia, this is Tom. Tom, Felicia.'

"'Hey, amigo. Got snapper tonight. Your favorite,' said Tom.

"A squeeze of the arm, a glance of anticipation.

"Ralph gave Felicia a paperback copy of *Love in the Time of Cholera*. 'See you on Thursday,' he said. And with a little movement of the head in the direction of Tom, 'I know I can count on you.'"

Lizzie and Nicola took a last sip of champagne. The bright sunshine no longer seemed so friendly.

"Have you ever been to the Keys, Randall?" asked Lizzie.

"Once or twice," he said with a wry smile.

"Oh, I see," they said together.

~ The Counselor's Tale ~

Moira

A counselor, gone prematurely gray,
Accompanies the party on its way.
She walks, unfit, perspiring in the heat,
Nods wisely, questions, never indiscreet.
A body waistless, clothes *désordonnés,*
Dry, wispy hair in casual disarray.
Her clothing style unchanged since she was twenty,
And not for lack of cash, for she has plenty.
Her native turquoise jewels clunk and clink,
A model of a *guru,* one would think.
An ornament to her august profession,
Anxiety she lightens, and depression:
"Say how you feel, whence does the problem stem,
I do not sit in judgment or condemn.
I'm here to listen, not dispense advice,
To give implicit pardons—for a price."

The next day we came to "Clairvaux," the Valley of Light
where St. Bernard established a new Cistercian monastery in
the early twelfth century.

"Rather a comedown from its glory days," said Nigel, gazing around at the tired, decrepit buildings.

"My guide book says it's now a home for the insane," added
Evelyn.

We explored the courtyard, peered into the barred windows on the ground floor, and retreated along the alley by which we came. A disheveled inmate followed us.

"*Cinq francs pour Jésus,*" he called, "*cinq francs pour Jésus!*"

Moira gave him five francs, and he dropped back, watching us leave. Evelyn was walking with Moira and Darryl joined them.

"I'm glad they look after these poor people," said Moira. "Some disturbed people survive out in the community, but mostly they end up on the street, homeless alcoholics or drug abusers."

"Have you done any work with mental patients?" asked Darryl.

"No, like a lot of counselors, I don't treat people with serious personality disorders. My specialty is the upper middle class client with low self-esteem."

"Do you have any good counseling stories?"

Moira knew a tale was expected, and she was prepared.

"It's unethical to talk about our clients, but there is one story I can tell you, about a fellow counselor I was friendly with."

"Her name was Carrie Ann Holland. Like myself, she had a practice in West Palm Beach. It's a town full of rich, dysfunctional families who have everything that makes life comfortable, and little that makes it happy. Most of our clients live in these pseudo-Spanish, ranch-style bungalows with two or three cars in the driveway. All you hear is the hum of lawn-mowers and the plop of bodies in the swimming pool."

Evelyn and Darryl smiled, as if they knew the scenario all too well.

"Carrie Ann and her husband, Jim, were originally from Ohio, but Jim moved his young company down to Florida to take advantage of the weather and the golf. Carrie Ann had trained to be a counselor, but she only took on clients after she and Jim came to Florida. That's when I met her. I supervised her work, even though we were about the same age, and we became friends.

"One thing you need to understand is that despite their wealth and privilege, many women in West Palm Beach have a poor self-image. The children have usually left home and visit their parents infrequently. The husbands are preoccupied with money and are often workaholics. Even the retired men spend their days reviewing their investments or getting involved in the local country club. The women are alone much of the day, just hoping they'll get a bit of attention from their husbands in the evenings.

"A crisis develops when husband and wife stop sleeping together. I have my own name for it: 'second stage empty nest.' It happens often, partly because the houses are big and it can be convenient to have your own bathroom and closets."

"It could also be convenient if your husband snores," said Evelyn.

"Or if your wife wants to avoid sex. Some women prefer to ration their affections just enough to stop their husbands from complaining," added Darryl. He saw the amusement in the faces of the women and added, "Or so I'm told!"

"True," said Moira, laughing, "there are lots of reasons. But I always advise against it. People don't realize how important sleeping together is to a happy marriage. Of course, physical closeness guarantees nothing, but the lack of it, the end of intimacy, can be a fast track to emotional disengagement and divorce. Anyway, the separate-bedrooms decision is one of those moments in life when distressed middle-aged wives choose to visit a counselor.

"Carrie Ann made quite a niche for herself in West Palm Beach counseling such women. She explained the importance of not going to sleep angry with your partner and keeping the sexual side of marriage alive and kicking. She often shared some of her own experiences, explaining, for example, how she and her husband overcame 'relationship drift.'

"I suppose it's natural to assume that someone providing marriage counseling has a successful marriage herself, and I took it for granted in the case of Carrie Ann. I knew that Jim was driven in business and passionate about golf. But it never crossed my mind that the golf widow might be discontented.

"And then suddenly, Carrie Ann announced that she was moving to Chicago. Why? Were she and Jim separating after so many years? Despite our friendship, she seemed unwilling to talk about it, and I was truly upset. She seemed in a world of her own, not in the mood for reason or discussion. She never mentioned golf or accused Jim of infidelity, nothing like that. I felt sad. It's hard to make friends at our age and tough to see them leave town.

"Several months later, I had a phone call from Carrie Ann. She was coming to West Palm Beach on business and wanted to get together. She said she needed some informal advice, and I invited her to lunch. She showed up at my house, red-eyed and tense. I thought her fatigue seemed extreme for a three-hour flight from Chicago; clearly, she was under stress. As we sat down for a Bacardi and orange juice, she started her story.

"She began by talking about her cleaning lady who had been with her for ages. Carrie Ann told me that Mrs. Rodriguez, whom I'd met several times, had come from a lower-middle-class neighborhood of Havana, but her son was smart and went to medical school there. When he received his degree she fled with him to Miami in a rickety fishing boat across eighty miles of ocean.

"Mrs. Rodriguez had her own way of working that involved turning the house upside down. She would flit from room to room dusting here, polishing there, and vacuuming in a welter of cords, nozzles, dust cloths, buckets, and multicolored bottles of cleaners. And she would sing along with the radio, which she played at full volume. Everything seemed to amuse her. She chuckled when Carrie Ann showed her the precise spot where the kitchen sponge should be kept, at the back of the sink. She grinned when Carrie Ann insisted that the dining room chairs be placed just so, at equal intervals around the antique dining room table. And she giggled when Carrie Ann asked her to position the flowers on the coffee table, precisely in the middle. Carrie Ann admitted that she was irritated by her cleaning lady's lack of attention to detail.

"To keep out of the way, Carrie Ann would escape to her office in the back of the house, where she talked to her clients about self-esteem. She would then return to the house for lunch and see Mrs. Rodriguez doubled up with laughter at some unexplained joke on the Spanish language radio frequency."

"You must have wondered what Carrie Ann's former cleaning lady had to do with her new life in Chicago," said Darryl, as he passed around some trailmix.

"I did, but I've learned from many years of counseling that it's important to let people tell their stories in their own way. So we moved on to lunch, and I let Carrie Ann continue. As she put it, Mrs. Rodriguez's routine was unremarkable, except for one thing. In all the time she worked for her, she never seemed to grasp the fact that Carrie Ann's surname was 'Holland.' When she arrived on a Tuesday morning, the conversation would go like this:

"Carrie Ann: 'Good morning, Mrs. Rodriguez.'

"Mrs. Rodriguez: 'Good morning, Mrs. Bolan. . . .'

"Carrie Ann: 'It's a nice day, isn't it?'

"Mrs. Rodriguez: 'Oh eet is, eet is.'

"Then, in the evening, Carrie Ann would pay Mrs. Rodriguez, always in cash, for she never paid household employment taxes, and ask after her son, the doctor. As Mrs. Rodriguez walked out the door, the conversation would go like this:

"'Goodbye, Mrs. Rodriguez.'

"'Goodbye, Mrs . . . er . . . Bolan.'

"'Take care now.'

"'Si. Si. Good night.'

"And apart from Carrie Ann's repetitive reminders on orderliness in the house, that would be the sum total of communication between employer and employee.

"Carrie Ann said she asked her husband Jim one day why he thought Mrs. Rodriguez couldn't get their name straight.

"'I have no idea!' said Jim. 'Perhaps it's a little game.'

"Carrie Ann, as a counselor, knew all about games people play. She knew, for example, that one way to promote your self-esteem was the 'I've got you, you son of a bitch' ploy. It made you feel in control. Carrie Ann would discuss such psychological game playing with her clients, but she never gave much thought to Mrs. Rodriguez. Her husband's comment about 'a little game' passed underneath her radar screen.

"Carrie Ann put the confusion down to poor English, but nevertheless, she always left some mail addressed to 'Mr. and Mrs. Holland' on the front hall table with the hope that Mrs. Rodriguez might spot it and realize her mistake.

"From time to time, Carrie Ann told me, she would give a dinner party, and Jim, who normally kept to more serious topics, would tell their guests about their Cuban cleaning lady and how, after more than a decade, she still hadn't grasped their surname. He would address Carrie Ann as 'Mrs. Bolan' across the table, and everyone would laugh.

"'Where did she get that particular name?' someone would invariably ask. It was a mystery.

"As time went on, Mrs. Rodriguez's eyesight deteriorated, and the standard of cleaning declined. She remained cheerful as ever, but it was clear that she would have to stop working. The Hollands gave her a generous lump sum to help her in retirement. Mrs. Rodriguez wept a little tear and said a few heartfelt words of gratitude. The Hollands bade her farewell and shortly thereafter hired a Nicaraguan immigrant.

"Carrie Ann then told me about a phone call she received three years later. The man said he was phoning with bad news about Gloria.

"Gloria? thought Carrie Ann. *Who's Gloria? The maid's name is Maria.* She was thinking, naturally, of the Nicaraguan immigrant.

"'The family is so grateful for the kind and decent way you and your husband treated my mother,' said the caller. 'But I'm sad to tell you that now she has passed on. The funeral is next Friday.'

"'I'm so sorry to hear it,' said Carrie Ann, realizing that the caller must be Mrs. Rodriguez's son, the doctor, calling to say his mother had died.

"So sad, thought Carrie Ann. *I must go to the funeral.* Her husband accompanied her.

"They eventually found the church, on the outskirts of town.

"'Do you think this is the right place?' asked Jim. He parked the car and crossed the road to look at the church notice board. 'Funerals,' it said, '11 A.M.: Gloria González. May her soul rest in peace.'

"Jim returned to the car. 'What was that address again?' he asked.

"'2200 Christoforo Colón.'

"'Well, it says González on the board over there, not Rodriguez. Are you sure you wrote it down correctly?'

"Carrie Ann crossed the road with her husband to look inside the church, and before they could decide what to do, they were escorted to a pew.

"'We can't leave now,' said Carrie Ann. 'Let's make the best of it.'

"Carrie Ann described to me the joyful, energetic service that contrasted with the dour solemnity of funerals she had known. The service was in Spanish and interspersed with singing and live guitar. The men and women who stood to eulogize the departed spoke respectfully but cheerfully, lacking the strained, anxious looks of those from her own depression-prone community. Afterwards, the mourners filed into a sun-lit churchyard where they greeted each other with animation. A middle-aged man approached the Hollands. With slightly graying hair, he looked distinguished and he spoke excellent English. Carrie Ann blushed as she told me of their first encounter. He was very attractive.

"'You must be Mr. and Mrs. Holland. How nice to meet you at last. My mother would have appreciated your coming.'

"'She was a lovely person, so reliable. We'll never find another like her,' replied Carrie Ann.

"The doctor paused reflectively. 'She had a great sense of humor. In her youth she was a wonderful storyteller. She could be very funny.'

"'You know,' said Carrie Ann, 'she always called us "Bolan." Fifteen years! We grew to like it.'

"'Yes, I know. It was her little joke. And you always called her 'Rodriguez.'

"'So your name really *is* González?' asked Carrie Ann, embarrassed.

"'She used to say, "maybe in my next life I'll come back as a Rodriguez, the rich and famous Gloria Rodriguez!" We used to laugh about it when she told the story. My mother found humor in everything around her.'"

"So Mrs. Rodriguez was making fun of Carrie Ann and her husband all the time," commented Darryl.

"It seems that Mrs. Rodriguez—sorry, Mrs. González—had discovered a quicker road to self-esteem than Carrie Ann had been able to offer her clients. Faced with the Hollands' apparent inattention both to her and to her correct name, she made a joke of it.

"In the days that followed, Carrie Ann would reflect on her advice to clients. Typically, she organized support groups on self-esteem or suggested her clients treat themselves to a new outfit or a bottle of perfume to boost their spirits. But maybe Mrs. González's approach to life was a more healthy one from a psychological point of view. Maybe she should be helping her clients discover humor and lightheartedness.

"'Please, Mrs. Holland, Mr. Holland, let's not worry about the past,' said Dr. González. 'Come share our celebration of my mother's life.'

"So Carrie Ann and Jim went from the church to the family wake. Mrs. González's whole neighborhood had turned out to say goodbye. Black, brown, and white—all dressed in their Sunday best—danced to the beat of a live Cuban salsa band. Tables groaned with local seafood and the drink flowed. It was thirty years since Carrie Ann had attended such a joyous, uninhibited gathering. Through the throng appeared Dr. González, who bowed, a playful smile on his lips. He held out his right hand.

"'Mrs. Holland, may I have the honor?'

"Carrie Ann demurred at first, looking inquiringly at Jim. But Jim shrugged his shoulders grumpily and looked at his watch. He was probably thinking about the Open being broadcast on the sports channel.

"That was the beginning of the affair between the elegant, handsome doctor and the anxious, conscientious counselor.

"Suddenly, she was unavailable at her home office or on her cellphone. Suddenly, she discovered clients who required her to visit them, rather than the reverse. At one point, she had a minor car accident driving through a shopping area south of West Palm Beach, and her husband Jim asked her what on earth she was doing there. She never told me her answer.

"Of course, I had noticed, as had Carrie Ann's other friends and neighbors, that she was difficult to contact. But we would have been amazed to learn that while Jim was away attending trade conventions or competing at golf tournaments, she would meet the doctor at a small hotel south of West Palm Beach and check in as 'Mr. and Mrs. Bolan.' They both enjoyed the joke.

"By this time Carrie Ann and I had finished lunch, and we moved into the sunroom. I remember this because I took the opportunity to interrupt her.

"'Why?' I asked her. 'Jim was a decent man, and you had a successful counseling practice. Why give all that up?'

"'It's the puritan thing,' she told me.

"'Are you serious?' I asked.

"'I suddenly realized I'd bought into the puritan ethic at my mother's knee,' she replied, laughing. 'All work, no play, chase the dollar night and day. As a result, I suffered for years from acute generalized anxiety disorder, mixed with periods of depression. Why, you ask? We were well off, bored and frightened. Yes, frightened. Frightened we'd lose our money, frightened the neighbors wouldn't like us, and frightened of sharing our real thoughts with each other.'

"'And an affair was the answer?' I asked.

"'Moira, it wasn't just an affair, it was a way of life, an attitude of mind. I didn't want to spend the rest of my life looking after a taciturn golfer and making small talk to the neighbors. I wanted companionship and fun.'

"It seems it was other things as well. The sex was terrific, she said. And she and the doctor would talk for hours about serious matters—sensitivities, vulnerabilities, and longings— that she had seldom discussed with her husband. She explained to the doctor how nervous she felt about being late for an appointment and how much she wanted to cure her need to get things done and just relax. She shared with him her fear that her daughter would marry her current boyfriend who, Carrie Ann thought, had a roving eye.

"The doctor, in turn, shared with her his love of music, his ambition to open a practice of his own and his longing to walk by the sea with her in Havana. And when they were all talked out, they would go dancing. Carrie Ann told me about laughing and dancing the rumba and the samba with wild abandon. She was smitten. She was in love.

"All those years she had been trying to find answers to her own problems while treating the emptiness and anxiety of others. And all the time her cleaning lady had the answer to her problems. She came to the house every week, but was barely acknowledged and kept at a distance. Neither woman had crossed the boundaries.

"So Carrie Ann left West Palm Beach. She boarded a plane bound for a new life with her handsome doctor, abandoning her husband and her constant introspection. In Chicago she attracted a new set of clients who, it turned out, shared the very same problems that had afflicted her clients in West Palm Beach: poor self image and relationship drift. The doctor joined a Chicago practice of internists caring primarily for Hispanic immigrants."

"It sounds like a happy ending. Why did she return to see you red-eyed and tense?" asked Darryl, intrigued.

"Well, it turned out that she had two problems. One was a personal problem, the other a professional one."

"What was the professional problem?" As an entrepreneur herself, Evelyn identified with the struggles of other business-women.

"Well, Carrie Ann went off to Chicago determined to see the funny side of life and convey this to a new set of clients. But she soon discovered why some counselors tend to deal in palliatives and avoid the deep-down character issues.

"People spend money on all kinds of things, besides counseling, to boost their self-image. They'll start collecting something ('get yourself an interest'), go to a health farm ('get fit') or treat themselves to a body massage ('relieve the stress'). And if those things don't work, they'll buy some Paxil to get through the day.

"But mention sense of humor and you're entering deep into a minefield. Everyone thinks he has a sense of humor, and it's a rare human being who'll concede its absence. So when Carrie Ann began telling her new rich and oh-so-serious clients to lighten up and laugh at themselves, she was met with looks of puzzlement. *Was she saying they didn't have a sense of humor?*

"Carrie Ann thought this reaction missed the point. She was sure that everyone *had* a sense of humor, even if it was temporarily hiding under a bushel. All she wanted to do was bring it out. She was trying to divert the attention of her clients from their natural acquisitiveness, competitiveness, and insecurity and give them a better balanced personal psychology.

"She fanned her clients' sense of the ridiculous, mocked posturing and pomposity, and recommended books, films, and plays that she thought would amuse and distract attention away from money and status. But her approach did not seem to produce the desired results. Her clients' reluctance to admit their chronic self-importance gradually eroded her confidence, and she slowly reverted to her former prescriptions."

"What was the personal problem?" asked Darryl, far more interested in the intimate life.

"The personal problem was lack of sleep. It seems that her proud, passionate Cuban went late to bed and needed little sleep himself. They seldom ate before ten, and by the time she had cleared the dishes, her eyelids were drooping. He, by contrast, had boundless energy. Nearly midnight, and the evening for him had just begun.

"'Darling, it's wonderful in the afternoon,' she tried to explain. 'I could make love with you every day in the late afternoon, but by midnight I'm drifting away.'

"It was no good. They were seldom home before eight, and then he liked to shower, have a drink, and talk over the day's events. Dinner revived him, and afterward he was ready for a relaxed and sensuous session of prolonged lovemaking.

"There was no doubting Carrie Ann's sexual awakening. She loved it, but when it came down to it, she loved it in respectable moderation. After all, she was from Ohio. The intensity, the physicality, the frequency—she had not been prepared for all that.

"'Look,' she said, 'I'm no longer twenty-one. I need my sleep, eight hours of it. Less, and I can't get through the day.'

"And then there was her susceptibility to cold. Carrie Ann wanted a bedroom temperature well over seventy degrees Fahrenheit, but the handsome doctor did not agree. Despite his Cuban origins, he preferred a cooler temperature. He laughed at Carrie Ann when she complained, and he opened the bedroom window on a cool Chicago night. 'Fresh air, my sweet! More beauty for my beauty.'

"Now according to Carrie Ann, as soon as she was sure he was asleep, she crept out of bed and closed the window. But in the morning, she was awakened by the cold air. There it was, half-open again.

"'It's all very well,' she told me, blushing, 'but one minute I'm, well, you know, too hot, and the next I'm freezing under the blankets. We've now had weeks of playing fresh air games and pretending the window mysteriously blows open or shut. What can I do?'

"In short, Carrie Ann, otherwise blissfully happy, was almost sick with fatigue and longed for the deep peace of a long night's sleep."

"What did you say?" asked Darryl.

"Frankly, I didn't know what to say," continued Moira, "but I felt sorry for Carrie Ann. She seemed to have lost her newly gained carefree persona and reverted to type. So I excused myself and went upstairs. I tied a bandanna around my head, put on an old shapeless shift, and slipped into some flip-flops. I grabbed a bucket and mop and confronted Carrie Ann.

"'Good morning, Mrs. Bolan. . . .'

"Carrie Ann laughed. 'Good morning, Mrs. Rodriguez. It's a nice day, isn't it?'

"'Oh eet is, eet is.'

"'Did I ever tell you my name was Holland, Mrs. Rodriguez?'

"'And did I ever tell you my name was González, Mrs. Bolan?'

"'How do I get any sleep with that son of yours, Mrs. González?'

"'That son of mine, just like hees father. I used to put a leetle something in his evening drink. Try bromide. The Army used to use eet. Calm him down, si?'

"'I can't do that, Mrs. González!'

"'Then put on an extra sweater, lie back, and enjoy eet.'

"'But I'm exhausted.'

"'Then don't get up in the morning. That's how eet is in Cuba. See clients in afternoon. My son, he make plenty-a money. I know eet.'

"'Maybe you're right,' responded Carrie Ann. 'My clients don't seem to benefit much from my counseling in any case!'

"'You be needing a regular counselor of your own if you get yourself so worked up.'

"'But I want to do what I think is right for the client.'

"'In old version of Bible, Lord says to Saul, "eet is hard for thee to kick against the pricks."'

"'Meaning?'

"'Some things are just too difficult, Mrs. Bolan, just too difficult.'"

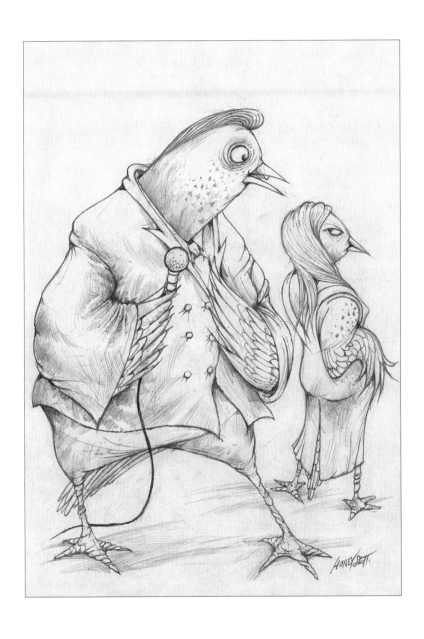

Jeremy

A talk show host! What kind of man is he?
Just smiling eyes and cheerful bonhomie?
He started life an actor in a troupe,
And found when young he could amuse a group
(On off days when the venue had gone dark
And they sat cold on benches in a park)
With monologues. And passers-by could see
An act like that should thrive upon TV.
And thus it did transpire that, quickly, he
Became a well-known personality.
In time he grew a shuttered, steely skin
To keep admirers out and feelings in.
And so, despite a friendly outer shell,
What is inside is grievous hard to tell.
He stays a mite apart, not talking much;
He seems to say "just keep away, don't touch."

Competitive salad making was a daily feature of this walk to
Rome. We had to eat, and good meals were expected. Early
every morning two members of the group, in turn, bought food
for the lunchtime picnic. This chore was a matter of pride to
those involved, and the picnic lunch had become a daily high-
light, as each pair of preparers sought to impress the group
with imaginative uses of food and wine, obtained from local
sources.

We settled for lunch under the pine trees by a tumbling Jura stream and waited while Jeremy and Lizzie arranged the dishes. The air was chilly after the heat of the lowlands, and several of us had donned our anoraks for warmth. High above us two hawks circled, wings outstretched, scanning the rocks and the thinning trees. Then Jeremy called us to attention, flourishing a checkered cloth, a twinkle in his eye.

"Ladies and gentlemen, today, for your delectation and delight, we have a wine—rich, supple, and full-bodied. I'd like to tell you that it's local, but in fact it cost thirty francs and comes from the lower slopes of the Andes. You will note that the lemons are from Orange and the oranges from a wooden crate marked 'California.' Let me point out the *pièce de résistance,* a mushroom and white anchovy salad prepared by my assistant, Lizzie."

With his free hand, Jeremy waved a flat tin, its lid rolled back.

"These white anchovies have a piquant flavor unique to this part of France and were hand-caught in the local *supermarché.* You may have heard Lizzie prowling around in the forest behind the hotel in the early hours of the morning. She found an amazing variety of mushrooms, which we have included. She *thinks* they are edible. Enjoy."

"Perhaps Lizzie would like to try them first," commented Nigel. "Otherwise, you may lose your entire audience."

"Did you know that Jeremy has his own radio talk show in London?" asked Lizzie, thrilled to be on holiday with a media personality.

"Well, yes, we call them 'chat shows,'" said Jeremy. "But most of the time I entertain small groups, fundraisers, that sort of thing. The British like irony, so I make up quirky monologues. You know, tongue-in-cheek stuff."

"Such as?"

"Oh, there's one about a nervous driver on a motorway and one about a New York traffic cop on vacation in London. Then there's the story about the old-age pensioner with a video recorder."

"Let's hear one," said Nigel.

At that moment one of the hawks high above swooped down upon some unsuspecting prey.

"What *are* those birds?" asked Lizzie.

"Peregrine falcons," replied Gerald, looking attentively through his army-issue field glasses. "Yes, peregrines, they're a favorite of falconers because they're so fast."

"That reminds me," said Jeremy. "I have a bird monologue, reminiscences of a sedge warbler. Would you like to hear it?"

We all nodded and Jeremy began.

"Out of the nest, pecking, dawn to dusk. I know we're known for our song, and it's true, you can hear us *chuck-chuck, churrr-churrr, whistle, trill,* but it's pecking we mostly do. And these days every bird is trying to find his own worm.

"Originally, sedge warblers divided up responsibilities. The males did most of the out-of-nest work: pecking, marking out territory, watching for families of grubs out for an afternoon stroll. The females looked after the youngsters, gave them flying lessons and prepared tasty snacks for lunch—juicy items like stewed caterpillar or minced *ver vivant*. Females are best at that. It's what nature intended.

"But then the old rules were thrown out. The females started to go out foraging themselves. Off they'd fly into the reeds and marshes by the water's edge, gone for the day. No one wanted to appear old-fashioned, so soon they were pecking about just like the males. That's what I don't like about your average sedge warbler. Can't be the odd bird out.

"Mind you, the males weren't free from blame. Young sedge warblers used to find mates from their own neighborhood, no further than a copse a mile away. But then they started to fancy lady birds from backward places like Somerset and got carried away by the olive-brownglow of their feathers or the tone of their song. I remember a young male returning one day with a female *moustached* warbler. Now I ask you, a moustached warbler! Yes, they have some good tunes, but they also have a different dialect, different customs, and *no* manners. What's wrong with our own warblettes, I ask you?

"Diversity, the Sylviidae Council called it. I think the old fellows on the Council went along with diversity because they enjoyed ogling exotic warblers. Well, they could be real delicate and sexy. Amenable and subservient as well. It's disgusting! Sex mad, that's what they were, wondering what it would be like, how they'd respond, would they give squeaks of joy and all that.

"Now where was I? Ah, yes, no one exercised self-control any more, they just chased around after skirt. Sometimes these old-timers took up with foreigners themselves and left their own lady birds, something I deplored. I'd say to the old birds, 'Shame on you, it's adultery, that's what it is.'

"To be fair, I don't think many of our own lady birds did the gurgling and gasping bit anymore. They were constantly on the go, you see. Too busy. It was all 'Get on with it and let me lay these eggs.' You couldn't blame the males, in a way.

"Well, with the lady birds pecking around outside the nest, the adults stopped communicating. The familiar daily conversations in the bird world—'Is the nest-keeping too much for you, dear?', 'Do you feel an egg coming on?', 'Is baby chick clear of fowl-pest yet?'—were all abandoned. And parents found they had no time for the kids. Young sedges weren't getting early guidance or training for flock life. They felt isolated, with no one to tell their troubles to. They were getting into mischief, 'bigging it' in the willow thickets with their teenage warblettes, darting in and out of the dense vegetation, and chasing harmless reed warblers. If you protested, you were told, 'Get with it, man. It's every bird for himself nowadays!' Fortunately, I understood the growing need for moral guidance and decided that if I didn't defend the old values, nobody would. Something had to be done.

"I knew you had to sell behavior to the young the same way you sold bugs, worms, and nest materials to adults. The old warbler values of marital fidelity, respect for your elders, and helping around the nest had to be made cool again. So I devised a marketing plan. I had advertisements and banners prepared, with moral messages such as 'A bird in hand is worth two in the rushes,' 'Every chick made is an egg to be laid,' and

'Warbler values are winning values.' It's true. We are the greatest breed of warbler in all the world. God's warblers. Sedge warblers.

"And I hit on the idea of the *Sedge-in-the-Hedge* club. I suppose you'd call it a youth club. It was the first ever. I'm a bit of an innovator on the quiet. The concept was to get a small panel of young sedges together on a Tuesday evening. None of your intellectual types, just birds with genuine problems. Then I'd bring in a couple of bird psychologists, 'sedge-psychos' I called them, to give the show credibility.

"So here's how my youth sessions worked. I'd get the young birds to sit on the hedge, facing the audience on the ground, with the sedge-psychos perched on a low-hanging branch. Then I'd walk around with the mike and make sure each bird gave his or her name before offering an opinion. The young sedges received advice on relationships, feathercare, petting and so on, and by and large, they listened attentively and appreciated it. We offered short, snappy bits of advice. A pithy bit of wisdom is as much as a warbler can handle. By the way, the size of a warbler's head bears no relation to the size of his brain. I've known tits with more brains than your average sedge warbler.

"It was amazing how quickly the youngsters discovered that their problems were shared by others in the flock. The idea was to get the young birds thinking about a sedge other than themselves. Of course, most of the participants were warblettes. They like discussing their problems with other females. So what's new? The young males soon cottoned on to the fact that the good looking young virgins came to these sessions to pour out their problems, and they started turning up, trying to attract a mate. They would stand on the low branches and sing their hearts out, *chuck-chuck, churrr-churrr, whistle, trill,* getting louder and louder, drowning out the questions and the answers. It wasn't that they deliberately wanted to be disruptive. In fact, they were surprised to discover that females had any problems at all.

"So I thought to myself, let's turn this to advantage. I announced that *Sedge-in-the-Hedge* would be expanded and that every Thursday evening there would be a singles' show. Males could go through their wooing routine, just like the old days.

"As the organizer I compèred it, of course. The trick was to let the young male sedges compete for attention. As you know, the more competition there is, the more elaborate the bird-song. I gave three minutes to each of the lads. The warblettes screamed and blew peck-kisses. I don't know why they have to scream. It lets off energy, I suppose.

"Every type of song, phrase, and elaborated repetition was represented, and on all imaginable themes. We had impersonations of every breed of bird for miles around, and the quality of the singing was awesome. The males sang as they came in the door and sang as they left, with or without a warblette. There was the usual jostling and mock fighting you'd expect with a group of male birds, each trying to be cock of the roost. My achievement was to get these youngsters to promise, in public, to love, honor, and obey, just like their old grand-warblers.

"My sessions at *Sedge-in-the-Hedge* were a success and I became a personality around the marshes. I acquired my own personal groomer and worm harvester and had a lot of leisure time, time for a fluff of the feathers or a couple of hours sunbathing. Naturally, my wife stayed at home to look after me and the fledglings. She complains, you know, but basically she's a good woman. I would lie back and eat dead bugs in the sun, dark glasses over my eyes. That's the life, I tell you!

"But I was far from idle. I was part of a political action group that favored equitable taxes. I didn't see why the Council Tax on my nest should be higher than the one on my neighbor's nest, simply because I was more successful. Some birds argued that richer families should pay higher taxes than others. That was unfair. Fortunately, I was supported by Vers Galliques Ltd., an importer of gourmet French worms. They wanted the right sort of bird elected to the Sylviidae Council, and they chose me.

"Unfortunately, I had some enemies. There was this liberal crowd that constantly whinged, calling me an extremist and claiming I was intolerant and against lady bird rights. Complete nonsense, of course; I love the ladies. Wouldn't do a thing against them. It was all political, this opposition. Just envy, but enough to prevent my election to the Council on several occasions.

"Meanwhile, the *Sedge-in-the-Hedge* club grew in popularity, and I hired an assistant to do the organizing while I gave press interviews and made videos of my life. Two biographies were written about me, and I couldn't leave the nest without having to sign autographs. It was good to have the community recognize me. I like to think I made a difference.

"Responding to public demand, I expanded the scope of the *Sedge-in-the-Hedge* program to give the flock an opportunity to discuss their goals in life and to offer advice to guest visitors about good worming areas and local services. I dispensed with the sedge-psychos and just used sedges with common sense.

"That's how I met Josephine. One day she just showed up for the Friday noon show. I was stunned. I couldn't tweet. For months I'd been surrounded with bright-eyed young females scratching messages in the soil for me, sending me anonymous worms, mincing, sidling, even cooing like those ridiculous white doves. I had totally ignored them, of course.

"But Josephine was different, not some gauche young thing who could only, like, *chuck-chuck, churrr-churrr, whistle, trill.* This was a lady bird of the world. Her breast feathers were of a rich, rust color with a deep, dark center. Her throat and breast were covered with the most exciting dark spots.

"It isn't polite to look at a lady bird's underneath unless you are married to her, but I sneaked a peek while she bent over to file her toenails. The feathers were a luxurious creamy white with the slightest tinge of red on the flanks. But it was her head and bill that set my heart thumping and cut my trill stone dead. Her crown was streaked in the richest olive brown, her feathers were of a healthy, glowing color, her lower mandible was a brilliant yellow, and there were brown markings down the side of the head towards her exquisite neck. She didn't squint but looked me right in the eye, frankly, with a slight smile around the beak. When she sang it was as if a choir of nightingales had gathered to serenade me.

"I knew immediately from her accent that this was no common *acrocephalus schoenobaenus,* no bog warbler. Josephine came from Italy, chic and elegant, not a feather out of place.

When she walked, she walked not like most warblers, with a slight lurch as the right leg moves forward to be followed by the left, but with a smooth, almost effortless glide. I noticed her groomed feathers. Some droplets sparkled on her wings; she had just finished a long, lazy bath in a nearby pond. I saw her cross her legs, not like most lady birds, whose claws stick out at ungainly angles, but neatly and elegantly.

"'Where on earth,' she asked huskily, 'can a bird get a decent feather grooming on this gloomy island? This rain's a disaster for a bird's coiffeur.'

"She? Need a coiffeur? This was style. I was in love. The audience tittered (excuse me, twittered). 'Ridiculous,' I heard a female say, 'what does it matter? Guys want a mate, not a runway model. I can't stand these affected continentals.'

"I knew it was jealousy. 'Come on, ladies,' I said, 'we can all learn a thing or two from our continental cousins. It's a matter of self-respect. Look good, feel good, that's what I say. A weekly grooming would benefit us all.'

"'Are you saying we look scruffy?' 'She has no monopoly on good looks.' 'She's just trying to steal our mates,' came voices from the audience.

"'What's the problem?' I asked. 'There are plenty of males to go around. We must be tolerant.' I was delighted to steal this small piece of liberal political correctness.

"But the audience ignored me. 'Go back to Italy!' they shouted. 'We don't need you here!' The auditorium erupted with the ladies' cat- (sorry, bird-) calls, as I hurried forward, appealing for calm. The mood was ugly. I gave a further homily on diversity and tolerance and hurried Josephine off the stage.

"That night she disappeared. I searched for her everywhere, in every tree, every garden, every hedgerow. I sent young males out into the sedge, calling her name. No sign of her. It had been disgraceful behavior on the part of the audience. Communities should always show hospitality.

"I left at dawn, secretly, flying solo. It can be dangerous without the flock, but a bird has to do what a bird has to do. I guessed she had headed south, back to Sorrento and the sunshine. *What was the truth behind this beautiful bird? Why did she speak Italian? Why did she live there rather than migrate like everyone else? Why had she come to Surrey?* I might never find her. It was a risk I was prepared to take.

"So, I left *Sedge-in-the-Hedge* and the youngsters in Surrey behind me. Yes, they looked up to me, but they'd be all right. Someone else could do their bit. It was my life, after all. The wife and the newborn chicks? Look, Josephine was there, there in Italy. I promised myself I'd never give up, not 'til she was mine.

"I crossed the Channel, flying high to avoid the attention of the gulls. They're big, and you never know. Sometimes migrating sedge warblers hit houses or lighthouses and die. They're the dumb ones, but you have to take care.

"Once I hit the French coast, I adopted the traditional pattern of flying at night and hunting for food during the day. I went over the Swiss Alps for speed. It was direct but dangerous. There are eagles who can remove your feathers before eating you and hawks who dive out of the sun and snap your neckbone in full flight. It was cold, and there were strange alpine plants and flowers and unusual worms and beetles—

food I wasn't used to. The air was thin, the going slow and exhausting, and by the time I got to the pass I was breathless and had to walk across the frontier. I had done it. I was determined, you see. A younger bird wouldn't have had the determination.

"Anyway, I was soon gliding down the valleys, resting in a sunny spot for a day, then on to the coast and plentiful food and warmth. Next time I'm going via Monte Carlo! (Incidentally, you'll soon be able to read my new book, *Songbird in the Alps,* published by Sylviidae Press and sponsored by Warblers for the Pound, price thirty-three elderberries.)

"I found Sorrento. I dare say you associate Sorrento with bluebirds. That's humans for you. Well, I'll tell you, it's not just bluebirds in Sorrento, no sir! I soon found a flock of sedge warblers. At first they were friendly enough, though difficult to understand. Most of them wintered in Egypt near the pyramids and kept going on about whether sand baths were good for feather glow and whether you found the best bugs in an ancient ruin. But as soon as I asked for Josephine, they turned their tail feathers in my face and flew away. I was on my own.

"A bird has sharp vision, so I sat on a bough and kept watch. At last I saw Josephine, giving a concert in the upper branches of a lemon tree. She moved up and down the hillside in a flowing fashion, singing her heart out, then launched vertically into the air with fluttering wing beats, turned rapidly, and descended in a slow spiral, her wings and tail outspread. The sound of her trill thrilled me, yet I felt a pang of disappointment. Josephine? *Chuck-chuck, churrr-churrr, whistle, trill,* just like any other sedge warbler? But at least I had found her.

"I wasted not a second. Up I flew, straight as an arrow.

"I wasn't a big wheel for nothing. Warblers are tough where I come from. So I flew—as fast as any racing pigeon, crossing the flights of smaller birds on the periphery and ignoring the alarm calls of the young males—straight at Josephine.

"'Josephine,' I called out. 'It's me. Come with me and be my mate.'

"'So you followed me,' she warbled. She looked distracted, uncomfortable. She wouldn't look me in the eye. 'We're just off to Capri. Meet my suitors!'

"Meet my suitors! There must have been a dozen of them. Huge they were, and tough, with mean beaks. Competition was one thing, and I can hold my own, but they came for me, mobbing me. Soon the whole flock joined in the mêlée, birds zooming, colliding, squawking, screeching, a mass of claws and falling feathers, a sort of avian Battle of Britain, only it was me against all the others.

"I'm quick and can turn on an elderberry. At home I'm known as the fastest, most nimble flier in the flock, not just a good-looking hunk with exceptional probity, although I'm that too. My trip south had hardened me, left me lean and fit. Man, was I fit, not like these effete birds, breeding in Italy, with their easy feeding and relaxed drinks by the sea at sunset. 'Gucci warblers,' I call them, and for a while I gave them hell! Males dropped from the skies. I positioned myself between two attackers and skipped out of the way at the very last moment, so that one ugly male was impaled on the beak of the other. I dive-bombed the main suitors while they flapped around trying to spot me. If I could chase them off, the rest of the females and younger birds would be no problem.

"But I was outnumbered. A particularly tough-looking male attacked me. I felt a sudden pain in my right wing. *Was it bruised or broken?* I lost speed and height. Suddenly, Josephine was close by.

"'You and me?' I gasped.

"'Take my advice, get the hell outta here. Ci vediamo!'

"'Come back with me to England. I can't live without you.' But she had gone.

"It was too late. A Surrey sedge warbler is one tough avian, but not even I could handle a head-on attack by over twenty angry male warblers, even if they were foreigners. My damaged wing was useless. As I lost altitude, I felt more jabs, as vicious beak thrusts pierced my feathers and forced me earthwards.

"I must have lost consciousness, because I woke several hours later, my wing in pain and broken feathers all over me. Otherwise, I had survived. I rested up for two weeks, hiding in a thicket. Gradually, I recovered. Taking it in easy stages and moving only at night, I flew home, agonizing over the loss of Josephine. How could she have rejected me? She was so beautiful. I've never wanted another bird as much.

"Then my wing started giving me trouble again. It was hard work over the mountains, and I was breathless and tired. I began to feel more and more angry. Who the hell did she think she was, this Josephine? Turning up in Surrey, criticizing the flock, the weather, and the countryside? She'd led me on with those come-hither eyes and fancy feathers. She had lured me into a trap, that's what, a trap. She knew I'd follow her, and she had her mafiosi lying in wait for me. I'd been assaulted, battered, my wing bruised and nearly pecked to death, just for her pleasure. Her hoodlums wouldn't dare attack our whole flock. No, they picked on me because I was the leader of our community. I'd been nice to Josephine, welcoming. To hell with her. As one of the lady birds said, 'Guys need a mate, not a runway model.'

"I began to hurry, flying longer and faster. I wanted to get home.

"'Where have you *been*?' my wife demanded. 'I was so worried. We've been looking for you everywhere. The *Sedge-in-the-Hedge* club has postponed their sessions. They're waiting for you.'

"Tired and bedraggled, and without the benefit of even a cursory puddle-bath, I called a meeting. Most of the flock showed up and a hush descended as I made my entrance. Words were being exchanged behind raised wing feathers.

"'Lady birds, warblers, and fledglings,' I began. 'You see before you the subject of a heinous attack, an attack so sneaky and forceful that it must have been planned well in advance by a small group of highly motivated birds.'

"'Outrageous!' 'Scandal!' 'Tell us what happened!' they shouted.

"'A month ago,' I continued, 'I went out for an evening constitutional before perch time. It was getting dark. All of a sudden, I was set upon by a group of moustached warblers, hundreds of them, screaming like banshees. They attacked me, unprovoked, damaging my wing and forcing me to the ground. I struggled, of course, but was overwhelmed. I was tied to a sapling in the middle of a thicket, without food, water, or medical help. One of my jailers called me "the son-of-a-feather-less-hen." "What shall I do with him, Carlo," he called to an accomplice, "peck out his eyes?"

"'Yes, you've guessed it. They were foreigners! And why should they attack me, unprovoked and without warning? Jealousy, my friends, jealousy. They are envious of our way of life.

"'They roughed me up and tortured me. But it takes more than that to finish off a sedge warbler from Surrey! I managed to escape. I was desperately injured, as you see, but I got away. And I'm here to warn you, all of you.'

"I dragged my right wing across the ground, looking as pathetic as possible.

"'This,' I told them, 'is a serious situation. At any moment we may be attacked, our territory taken over, our nests robbed. We have become too tolerant, too laissez-faire. We must reintroduce pecking to death, to deter serious crime. A policy of three-strikes-and-you're-defeathered will eliminate vandalism and magpie-like theft from nests. And we must reintroduce the draft. It gives youngsters a sense of discipline and of working as a team in the community. Under the old, liberal regime it was every bird for himself, and to hell with the flock.

"'Will you stand around while strangers take your birthright? Will you let them carry off your fledglings into slavery or butcher them before your eyes? We must mobilize, plan, be vigilant! We must make our woodlands and meres safe for future generations. For this, the flock needs leadership!'

"The response was deafening. *Chuck-chuck, churrr-churrr, whistle, trill* was heard from all sides, and I was hailed as a savior. My election to the Sylviidae Council was assured. It was the right thing to do, that speech.

"And now? I've been the undisputed leader of the flock for years. I have my favorite roost, alongside the older males— eight serious birds in a row. As you know, when birds are roosting, the senior birds get the warmest and safest positions. But I have the biggest say.

"The morals of the flock have definitely started to improve, I'm glad to say. Teenage pregnancy's down, but the thing I'm most gratified about, long term, is the drop in the divorce rate. I always tell the *Sedge-in-the-Hedge* club, my political base: 'Honor your wife, be faithful, and remember, looks are only feather deep.'

"Yes, we're a fortunate flock, us sedge warblers. God has truly blessed us."

～ The Herbalist's Tale ～

Nicola

Nicola is priest and pontifex
To this, a tawdry world consumed with sex.
As balm to the old who anxiously de-brief,
She tenders tailored one-on-one relief.
Promoting obscure roots without misgiving,
She offers hope and thereby earns a living.
Yet, no cynic she, naïve, no guile,
An aesthete with a warm, inviting smile,
Which is her better part; for she is lean
And feeds like summer birds on seed and bean.
Angled is she in simple cotton shift,
Dangled her breasts, which sorely need a lift.
Without, she is a red-haired, green-eyed wraith;
Within, a soul with cherished dream and faith
That she will find from herbs, which she distills,
A cure for mankind's procreative ills.

Nicola moved ahead of the group across the mountain meadows leading to the Grand St. Bernard Pass, one of the five major passes through the Alps from Switzerland to Italy. Her long legs covered the ground with strong and graceful strides. From time to time she stopped and, with her spider-like fingers, picked a grass or wild flower and showed it to her companions. She knew its name, both Latin and common, and could describe its normal habitat and closest relatives. We delighted in the daisies, poppies, violets, orchids, campion and clover. Nicola pointed out the dog roses against the rocks and the isolated canterbury bells. Higher up we found mountain juniper and honeysuckle.

Lizzie gathered a bunch of dandelions and buttercups. They were familiar and plentiful.

"Do any of these flowers have medicinal uses?" asked Evelyn.

"Poppies, of course," replied Nicola. "Although it depends on the variety."

"I'm interested in herbal remedies, myself," said Evelyn. "Perhaps you can tell us something about yourself and your work."

Nicola paused a moment. "All right, I'll tell my story to the two of you, but not to the others. Like your story, Evelyn, it's too personal."

Lizzie stopped for a moment to tighten her shoelaces. Then the three women moved on and Nicola began.

"My mother lived in India as a young woman and learned about Indian and Chinese herbs, many of which grew near the house. On her return to England, she became an avid organic gardener and inter-planted vegetables with herbs, which provide natural protection from weeds and pests. I suppose I inherited my interest in plants from her. She took part in the annual village flower show and vegetable competition, and I remember she once won blue ribbons for three matching and perfectly shaped two-foot-long carrots and a tray of the whitest turnips of varying sizes.

"I was an only child, and my parents sent me away to a girls' boarding school on the south coast at an early age. I didn't mix much with the other girls. I was wrapped up in my own world, fascinated with stories of temples and Hindu gods. I read Kipling and, when I was older, Forster. Back at home on holidays, I used to talk to an old woman from the village who did our washing and ironing, a 'daily' we called her. She told me about remedies for common aches and pains, derived from herbs. I was intrigued by her knowledge.

"After school, I trained as a nurse. I worked hard, and avoided the parties and the hectic hospital social life. In the seventies, when nurses were so badly paid by the National Health, I looked for alternatives. I switched to contract work three days a week with a private agency, and that gave me time to pursue my interest in herbal medicine. I built up a card file on remedies, with tips and anecdotes as well as facts and medical research. I was largely self-taught, but I was conscientious and thorough, and it paid off.

"Around this time my father died, leaving some money to myself and my mother. I decided to start a small natural foods store in the Notting Hill area of London. It was the eighties and the early days of the health food craze. People had become more interested in natural foods and more confident in herbal remedies.

"My store was organized with the low-price bulk items near the door. Green and brown lentils, cannelini, and mung and borlotti beans were not going to attract the average passerby, so I minimized the risk of casual shoplifting. The cash register was also near the door, but my assistant did have to leave her post from time to time. Across from the beans were large bottles of vegetable juices—celery, carrot and beetroot—as well as a wide range of fruit juices. Then came the grains and cereals, and, next to them, the seeds, dried fruits and nuts, honeys and herbal teas. I sold a full range of books, too, covering the three main herbal traditions—Indian Ayurvedic, Chinese, and the Americas. I kept the higher priced herbal remedies in the back, where I set up my pharmacy.

"Like any good pharmacist, I gave free advice, and wrote out my prescriptions with rounded vowels and gothic consonants. A neat hand impresses a customer and looks professional. People consulted me on their sinuses, their joints, their nerves, and their bowels. Discretion was important.

"'I have a pain in my shoulder. It won't go away,' a client might begin.

"'I'm sure we can put that right,' I would say, calm and steady.

"'And,' the voice lowers to a soft whisper, 'I suffer from constipation and hemorrhoids.'

"'I'm sure we can put that right, too.' And I would recommend asparagus root for the arthritis and goldenseal for the digestive tract."

As Nicola paused, the three women noticed the skitter of alpine meadow larks in the hayfields and the distant sound of the alpine water as it rushed over the river rocks.

"After a year or so, I found I had a number of repeat customers, both men and women, and I began to become familiar with their ailments. Eventually, I built up relationships of trust, and my clients started to confide in me. It was sexual dysfunction that haunted them, or sometimes the sexual dysfunction of their partners. At first I would blush and ask myself, *Should I be listening to this?*

"But the need for advice on sexual performance was clearly there. So I arranged for a private consulting area in the stock room. Much of the lunchtime and afterwork hours I sat quietly, knees primly crossed, listening to customer laments about the most intimate aspects of their lives. Sexually naïve as I was, this became an absorbing pastime. I took to my customers' stories as I had to the tales of far off lands I had read as a child. And yet, when I look back on it now, their stories were not about glorious orgasms but about dismal encounters.

"Initially a client would give me an embarrassed, vague description, 'My partner's never "in the mood,"' or 'it's over too quickly.'

"I would say, 'Don't worry, I'm sure we can put that right.'

"'I've heard that wild yam and sarsaparilla are effective,' they might suggest. But I'm conservative and cautious with my prescriptions. I would explain the unwanted side effects of products like wild yam and prescribe a teaspoon of turmeric in green tea, firmly warning them against too much coffee or heavy meals. If this were not enough, I would prescribe one of the better known herbal remedies, such as ginseng. I insisted that the client return and give me a detailed report of the results, and I learned a lot about sexual preferences and activities from these conversations.

"My curiosity on the subject grew, and I decided to undertake a study of this field and to write a book I planned to call *The Sexual Effects of Common and Uncommon Herbs*. I felt this book would hold more interest if I could tell readers how and where the various roots, seeds, leaves, barks, and flowers were grown, and what claims were made for them locally. I could now afford to travel the world, possibly find some low-cost supplies and write it all off as a business expense against taxes.

"I had read Carlos Castañeda's descriptions of peyote, a cactus with a strong psychoactive effect, so my first trip was to Mexico, where I also learned about wild yams. Later I went to China, where I researched the varieties of ginseng and angelica roots and learned about the sexual impact of seahorses steeped in wheat liquor. My most extensive trips were to India, given my long-standing interest in the Asian subcontinent. But I also went to Africa to find out more about the bark from the yohimbé tree. The extract from this bark is known to help with erectile dysfunction, or impotence, but it also has numerous reported side effects, including high blood pressure and panic attacks.

"The more I traveled the more I learned, and the more products I was able to offer. I built up a little import business and sold some products to other herbalists and health food outlets."

"What about the book?" asked Evelyn, warming to Nicola's professional approach to her career. "Did you publish it?"

"No, I didn't. I was too busy. My clients were coming up with specific requests: to increase their stamina and endurance, to raise their sperm count, to stimulate their sexual fantasies, to heighten their orgasms, and so on. I was very client orientated and in the end I abandoned it.

"Well, you can imagine my excitement when I heard about a unique root, available in North Borneo, to enhance sexual desire and performance. This was only last year. It was an Indian herbalist who told me about it. He described it to me, but I could find nothing written about it in any of the herbal dictionaries or volumes on traditional medicine. So, I decided to go to Borneo myself. I knew this would not be an easy expedition so I allowed myself a month and left the shop in good hands.

"My main problem was to find a translator who was tactful and diplomatic, but at the same time sufficiently disciplined to translate precisely. I eventually found such a person through a British bank in Brunei. Her name was Yora. I didn't want to go into the jungle alone with a strange man.

"Yora made discreet inquiries about the root, but learned nothing. Then one day she arrived at the hotel, excited, saying she had heard of an old woman who dealt in the root, and who lived deep in the interior. We set off the next day, traveling through the rain forest in a canoe equipped with an outboard motor. We carried with us fuel, food, and water. It was hot and the river was swollen. We seemed to motor forever against the current, but eventually came to a wooden jetty and found our way to a longhouse deep in the forest. Longhouses are small villages built on raised platforms of logs or bamboo above the forest floor. We found the old medicine woman, seated on a mat, surrounded with the grizzled, shrunken heads of Dayak warriors. A long discussion ensued, but in the end she advised us to try elsewhere. So we got back into the canoe and paddled from longhouse to longhouse, but we didn't find what we were looking for.

"I was almost ready to give up when we got a clear lead about another old woman some twenty miles away, over the border in Kalimantan, near a logging camp. We made our way to her village. At first we were given the suspicious, silent treatment, but we persevered, sleeping in the guest hut, smiling often and eating with the old lady, slowly winning her confidence. Although herbal remedies were normally dispensed by medicine men, we learned that the 'homan' root, as it is called, is handled only by these old women in the interior of the island. It is very potent.

"The old woman eventually took me into her confidence. She explained that men from Europe and the subcontinent had come to Borneo asking about the 'homan' root over the last twenty years, but no one would talk to them. My unique advantage, it appeared, was being a woman, traveling with a female interpreter. The local Dayaks understood that such a powerful drug had to be strictly controlled, and thus each community had handed over responsibility for it to the local medicine woman. And by custom, the origin and processing of the homan root was kept a secret from the men of the tribe.

"'The root has been our secret for generations,' said the old woman through the interpreter. 'It is powerful and must be taken in only small doses. You must be careful to take the right amount. Too much and a man would need three wives! One old man deflowered forty-nine virgins at the rice festival after eating half a root. Traditionally, women will not take it because they fear it will cause them to be unfaithful and the consequences in our society for infidelity are severe. But women say their men are happy with it and continue far into the night.'

"I then inquired as to the precise nature and effects of the root. From what I could gather, it is a kind of narcotic, but its unique advantage is that it combines the soothing effect of a narcotic with the stimulatory effect of products that quicken circulation and boost the hormones, especially testosterone.

The effects depend on the size of the dosage, and vary from person to person. The old woman then outlined her methods for prescribing the root, emphasizing the need to take it a couple of hours in advance for maximum impact, and described the anticipated effects considering the size, age, and health of the client.

"I explained that I was a herbalist and researcher and asked if she would sell me some of the root. It turned out that she had just been on one of her periodic searches of the forest and had returned with a large basketful. 'What it is and where I find it are my secrets,' she said. I bought as much as she would allow and paid well for it. I put it out to dry in the warm sun and processed it, obeying the old woman's instructions. I then left Borneo, carrying with me a pale orange powder.

"On return to London, I checked again in my herbal books for some mention of this substance but could find nothing. This disturbed me, as it meant there was no known antidote, but I decided I could still prescribe it as long as I was cautious. After all, the village men had been using it for centuries. I felt an excitement about this product that I had not felt about other natural products, perhaps because I had been accepted into a secret society of women herbalists and perhaps because, if not the first, I was at least one of the first foreigners to acquire a substantial supply.

"Several of my customers knew about my trip and were anxious to try any new products. Among these was a young man who had fallen in love for the first time. He had never had sexual intercourse with a woman before and was terrified that he would not be able to perform. 'I'm sure we can put that right,' I told him, 'this will give you an erection for at least half an hour.' And I gave him, and subsequently others, a teaspoonful of the orange powder I had brought back from Borneo. In order to get another teaspoonful, I required a full report."

"And you got full reports?" Lizzie asked. "Honest reports?"

"Oh yes. And the powder seemed to have the desired effect. Mind you, I was aware of my own inexperience. I had had several relationships with men, well, flirtations, I suppose you'd call them. But they never got off the ground."

"People actually told you face to face what happened in bed?" Evelyn insisted.

"You have to understand, it was vital for me to learn in detail about the effects of the homan root. You may have heard about the adverse effects some sex enhancers have on men with weak hearts. Well, I wanted to avoid that sort of problem. I try to be as scientific as possible."

"Did you ever try it yourself?" asked Evelyn.

"I'll tell you. One evening I was in the shop after closing time, checking the inventory and waiting for a delivery scheduled earlier in the afternoon. Omar, the son of my longest-standing supplier, arrived with several cartons of nuts and grains. I had been ordering from his father for years, and my relationship with Omar, who was helping out temporarily, was professional and correct. On this occasion, however, he paused a moment as he greeted me and looked me straight in the eye. My heart skipped. I had seen attractive men before, but not in the intimacy of an empty shop at sunset.

"Omar was taller than I was, and about fifteen years younger. He had broad shoulders and moved with confidence. He was wearing a blue shirt that set off his olive skin and black hair. He caught me off guard.

"Perhaps I should explain. Not only had I had a sheltered upbringing, but I was seldom invited out on proper dates as a young woman, even while I was working in the hospital. I'm not sure why, but I know that things that preoccupied other women—clothes and makeup—never interested me. I concentrated on my job. But as I became better informed, and listened to my clients talk about their triumphs and minor bedroom tragedies, my interest in sex was fanned. I suppose this accounted for the arousal I felt in Omar's presence."

Nicola caught Lizzie's eye and gave her a shy, almost apologetic, smile.

"Well, go on," said Lizzie said. "He caught you off guard. What did he say?"

"'It's late, I could help you stack the shelves.'

"And I replied, 'Very kind of you.' And so we set to work.

"'How's business?' he asked.

"'It's good,' I said. 'Especially the pharmacy.'

"'I've heard. People say you give good advice.'

"'I do my best.'

"As Omar handed me the packages of figs and apricots, almonds and hazelnuts, kasha and bulgar, he touched my hand. It was a warm, soft touch that left me feeling weak and vulnerable. The next thing I knew, Omar had asked me out. *Had he noticed my dilated pupils?* I thought.

"The next few days were an eternity. I looked constantly at my watch, waiting for the minutes to tick by. My customers asked for advice and I responded as if in a dream. For the first time in my career, I kept no records of what I advised or how much I provided.

"Finally the appointed hour arrived, and I closed the shop a few minutes early. I waited an hour and Omar eventually appeared with apologies. We grabbed a pizza on the way to the cinema and once inside he ate it with gusto. I couldn't eat a thing. The movie was an adventure set in New York City. Or at least I think it was. Although I pretended to watch the screen, my mind was on Omar. *Some men like an older woman. Maybe he's afraid to make the first move.* I put my hand along the side of my seat, wondering if he'd take the hint. *Maybe he works too much and doesn't know many women. Why else would he have asked me out?* I leaned my shoulder against his to let him know I liked being near him.

"As the film drew to a close, I felt panicky. I had not given him the signal he was waiting for. He saw in me what men all my life had seen, a lady made for the church or the parlor but not for the four-poster. A woman made of porcelain—too remote, too brittle, too fragile. I couldn't live the rest of my life like this. I had to do something. I had to take the initiative.

"So as we left the cinema, I complained that my head ached and I wasn't feeling well. I said I wanted to go home, but to make up for spoiling the evening, I would like it if he would come to my flat for dinner next week. He said he would.

"Over the next few days I vacillated between canceling the date and taking an aphrodisiac to help break through my inhibitions. I decided on the latter. Normally I would have a wide range of choice. But I had procrastinated, and aphrodisiacs requiring a gradual buildup over several days were no longer an option. I decided to go for the real thing, the homan root.

"They say this sort of thing happens to men around forty. Well, it happened to me, an intense feeling that time and youth were slipping away. Call it devil-may-care. Soon I'd be shopworn without ever having been tried on. Who would care, anyway? And wasn't it important to my research to have first-hand experience of the drugs I was prescribing?

"The agreed-upon evening arrived. I took off early from work, remembering that to get the maximum effect I would need to take the root two hours in advance of Omar's arrival. I prepared the homan root by mixing it with three parts chickpea flour and enough water to make a thick paste. I baked the tiny cakes for fifteen minutes. The dinner for Omar was ready. I lay back on the cushions and ate all three cakes in succession. I then put on some Ravi Shankar sitar music, lit some candles, and scattered my embroidered cushions on the floor. It looked like a harem. I massaged my skin with deer tongue and jasmine and put a few drops of cardamom in an oil lamp. I dressed myself in a gold caftan I had bought on a trip to Morocco, and I let my slightly graying red hair hang loose.

"I remember very little of what subsequently transpired. I know that Omar arrived. In my heightened state, he appeared to be dressed in robes of red and green brocade with a gold dagger at his side. His eyes sparkled like emeralds and his teeth shone like white opals. I remember calling him 'Pasha' and asking to see what he had underneath his robes. And then, as I felt his flesh against mine, I heard a long, deep laugh and had an image of being thrown to the ground in a swirl of garments and trampled by antelopes. And then Omar took me around the world in a hot air balloon, but as we touched down to earth I sensed an abrupt end to the music and the sound of a quickly closing door. And then nothing, until I woke the next morning."

"That's incredible!" exclaimed Lizzie. "What happened next?"

"I felt exhilarated by my first sexual experience, but embarrassed at the recklessness of it, the lack of control. Although I had traveled widely and talked to people about their most intimate concerns, my own life had been circumscribed. I had lived my life through others, like a child reading a storybook. And when I myself experienced the kind of event that so conflicted others, I was ill-equipped to handle it.

"Following that memorable evening, I thought of nothing else but Omar and our encounter. My longing to see him eclipsed any feelings of anger or shame. But I soon fell into an acute state of despair that lasted for weeks. With the help of St. John's Wort, catnip and borage teas, and a brisk thirty-minute walk in mid-morning, I gradually recovered. Strangely enough, I found a glass of cream sherry in the evening before bed to be a good remedy as well, although none of the traditional books mentioned this alternative."

"And Omar?" This was Evelyn.

"As you might guess, I didn't see him again. A different driver delivered the fruits and grains after that. One day he told me Omar's mother had been admitted to hospital. She was very sick and not expected to live long. 'Terminal cancer,' the driver said. I spent hours picking out the right card to express my sadness at the news. I sent it to Omar but heard nothing from him.

"Then one day, Omar's father, Ridwan, phoned me. He said he knew I advised on herbal remedies. Could he come for a consultation? Did Omar know his father had phoned me? Had he told Ridwan about our night together? I didn't think it was something a son would discuss with his father, but I wasn't sure. The father had never requested a consultation before.

"Ridwan and I had only done business by phone, but I recognized him the moment he walked through the door. He was shorter than Omar, but had the same confident bearing and direct gaze. I took to him immediately. He was smartly dressed, with manicured hands.

"Ridwan said his problem was lethargy. He had been under a lot of stress since his wife's death. The tension had caught up with him. He was listless and lacked concentration.

"'How's Omar?' I asked, sensing it would be less revealing to inquire than not to inquire.

"'Fine,' replied Ridwan. 'He tells me you've built up quite a business here. He says you have a good reputation.'

"'I'm sure we can put you right,' I said. 'Lethargy can have both psychological and somatic roots. On the physical side, you find a total of eight monosaccharides in our body's glycoproteins.' I had recently learned about the essential sugars.

"'Oh?' he replied. He looked perplexed.

"'A glycoprotein is just a simple protein containing a carbohydrate.' I rattled on nervously, putting a small barrier of science between myself and my patient. 'But it's necessary for the proper functioning of the human body and its immune system. You've probably heard of galactose and glucose. We find these sugars in our daily diet, but there are six other essential sugars, like mannose and fructose, that we often miss.'

"'You're a *very* knowledgeable lady. I like that in a woman,'" he said.

"Well, I prescribed the eight essential sugars for Omar's father, and I was more than amply repaid with a free delivery of prunes and dried peaches."

Neither Evelyn nor Lizzie was inclined to pursue Nicola's concern with essential sugars.

"Come on, Nicola," said Evelyn, "don't change the subject. We want to hear about the homan root!"

Nicola blushed.

"I'll tell you what happened. Several weeks after Ridwan's first consultation, he phoned me asking for a second consultation. On arrival the next day around closing time, he explained that he had regained his energy. In fact, he felt reasonably fit again, but he now had another problem. His wife had been sick for a long time, and he was now interested in a new, uh, social life. Of course, it had never been an issue before. He was, after all, the father of six sons!

"I knew that the loss of a loved one focuses the attention on death and the need to reaffirm one's own life force, so I was sympathetic to Ridwan's complaint.

"'I'm sure we can put that right,' I said. 'Each of the major herbal traditions has its remedies, which operate either by balancing and boosting the hormones or by improving overall circulation of the blood (the Viagra effect). We could try ginseng or shatavari in the former category and ginkgo biloba, saw palmetto, or sweet tea vine in the latter. But I think, given your level of fitness and your age, ashwagandha would be your best option. It's a more generalized tonic and helps to improve sexual function by regulating the adrenal glands. You're not on medication of any sort, are you?' He assured me he was not.

"We discussed ashwagandha in syrup form.

"'Have you nothing stronger?'

"'I want you to try the ashwagandha first,' I said firmly.

"'I understand,' he said, not entirely convinced. And then he smiled in that spontaneous, charming way that Omar also had.

"'Nicola, how long have we done business together? Ten years now, and I have never thanked you properly. Lovely lady, let me take you to dinner tonight. I know a wonderful Lebanese restaurant.'

"The resemblance to Omar was seductive. I felt the same chemistry with father as I had with son, a sense of excitement and reawakening.

"So yes, we went to the Lebanese restaurant. The food was good and the service excellent. Ridwan plied me with wine, and when the flower seller came to the table, he bought not a single rose, but a dozen. He conjured up the blue seas and the mountains of Lebanon, the olive groves and the clear brilliant light. He waxed lyrical over my eyes, and his mouth visibly watered as he inspected my modest décolletage. He clasped my right hand and told me about his youth. I recovered my hand but, as the sweet trolley was wheeled to our table, I felt a hand brush my thigh. My thigh!

"'Ridwan, you've always said you value my business,' I said. I was flattered, but embarrassed. It's an old trick, as you know, feigning shock you don't really feel. And he saw through it.

"'Nicola,' he said, 'I've enjoyed the evening. May I see you again?'

"'I'd like that. Do you have something in mind?' I asked, feeling a warm glow inside.

"'Let me make it a surprise. Wednesday week? Shall I pick you up at your place?'

"'Now, if the ashwagandha doesn't work,' I offered, 'there's always the homan root.'

"Ridwan's eyes lit up and I found myself becoming as expansive and helpful to him as I was to my regular customers. I told him about my trip to Borneo, about the canoe trip, the shrunken heads and the search for the mystery root. I told him about the way the homan root was controlled by medicine women, the secrecy and the fear of overdose. When I reached the part about the forty-nine virgins, Ridwan's eyes became saucers.

"'So may I have the homan root, in case the ashwagandha doesn't work?'

"The homan root is potent, and expensive," I said.

"'I can afford it,' said Ridwan.

"One must never take more than a teaspoonful. I'll give you a small portion to try.' I pictured Ridwan at the door of my flat, consumed with desire. 'For maximum effect,' I added, 'you should take it two hours in advance.'

"Ridwan paid the bill. We returned to the shop, which was in darkness. I carefully measured out a level teaspoon of the homan root and put it in a small envelope. I gave it to Ridwan as a present. After all, he had invited me to an expensive meal. I then measured out another level teaspoon, put it in a second envelope and placed it in my purse. If Ridwan had not got the message before this then surely he would have it by now.

"At this point the wine and the water got the better of me and I excused myself for a moment. On my return, Ridwan had left. I went to the counter to rewrap the homan root and return it to storage. There was a marked indent in the bright, pungent powder that filled the box. I was angry. This was theft! Yet, I could hardly call the police about the disappearance of a few teaspoons of powder."

"Did you think of confronting him privately," asked Lizzie, "and asking for the powder back?"

"Well yes, I did. But what could I do? Phone him and accuse him of stealing? He was a supplier, and I dealt with his company every day. Well, I decided to wait until the Wednesday week, the day we had agreed to meet. But he didn't show up."

"So what happened?" asked Evelyn.

"A few days later, I received a phone call from Omar telling me his father had died, suddenly. He said it was a mystery. He was fit for his age and had no previous history of heart problems. He said there would be an inquest and he wondered if I could throw any light on Ridwan's death. He knew his father had consulted me. The court would be contacting me, of course."

"What on earth did you say?" asked Lizzie, who suggested they stop by the side of the road while Nicola finished her story. They were almost at the summit of the pass and the wind was chilly, but they found some rocks and huddled together while Nicola continued.

"I asked Omar if he could tell me more about the circumstances; and he hesitated, clearly embarrassed. He said Ridwan died in bed with a woman. Apparently, he had started seeing her shortly after his wife died."

"How did that make you feel?" asked Evelyn.

"I felt betrayed," said Nicola. "I felt he had misled me and used me. And I felt I had probably been right in the past to live independently and avoid relationships."

"But, I mean, how did you feel about Ridwan dying like that? Was it the homan root?"

"I don't know. I certainly hope not. I told Ridwan not to take more than a teaspoonful at a time. It never occurred to me he would behave in such an irresponsible way. He didn't need to take it all at once. I wonder if that woman encouraged him.

"You have to be careful. The homan root can give a feeling of exhilaration even without a partner. I feel terrible about Ridwan, but I've learned a lesson. You can't always trust people. I now take precautions. I lock up all my potent herbal preparations in the store."

"And what about the inquest?" asked Evelyn. "What was the verdict?"

"Death by misadventure," replied Nicola, and there was a moment of silence before the three women moved on.

"I didn't go to the funeral," added Nicola. "This was something I couldn't put right."

∞

We reached and crossed the Grand St. Bernard Pass, where monks still pray in their isolated cells and come to the aid of trekkers lost in the winter snows. We passed the lake on the south side of the pass and then descended the Roman road into Italy, relishing the clear air and warm sun. News of the homan root spread among the group, and more than one person longed to ask Nicola about her discovery. But the story, and its dark ending with the untoward demise of Ridwan, seemed to make further reference to it, if not ghoulish, at least inappropriate. It was the forthright Evelyn who summoned up the courage to ask the question on everybody's lips.

"Nicola, I can't get your story out of my mind. The homan root. Whatever happened to it?"

"I stopped prescribing the homan root."

"There's none of it left?" asked Evelyn.

Nicola smiled enigmatically. There was an uneasy silence.

"Just look at that view. Isn't it wonderful?"

The yellow mountain anemones and gentians were in full bloom and had moved their heads to face the sun. A jet passed silently by, leaving a vaportrail in the crystal clear sky above.

~ The Small Businessman's Tale ~

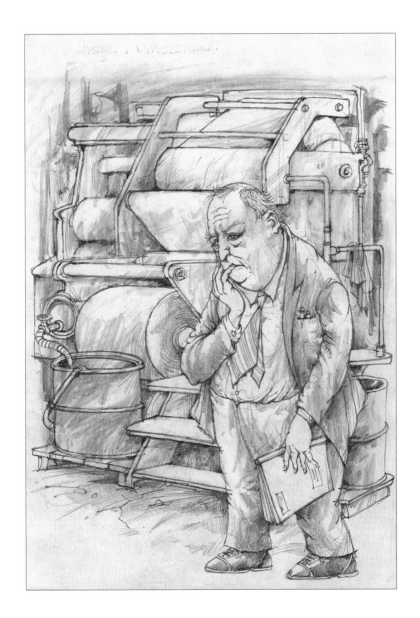

Richard

Some months ago he sold his family firm,
Before the worry rendered him infirm.
His hairless head has caught the July sun,
And, gleaming red, looks cooked and overdone.
His worry shows with bags below his eyes;
His constant nibbling's thickened up his thighs.
Beneath his midriff (just a pseudonym!)
He shows a subtle bowing of the limb,
So when he walks he sways from side to side
And bites his lip and sighs, preoccupied.
He has a friend, but cannot override
His fear of weddings and a lifelong bride.
And so he dithers, is it yes or no?
He must decide, or maybe see her go.
This stress destroys his quietness and his calm,
His steady hand's become a sweaty palm.

And then we arrived at the walled city of Lucca. Lucca was
an Etruscan town and then a Roman one and was the princi-
pal city in Tuscany in the ninth and tenth centuries. It is now
the attractive market town of a rich agricultural region. Nigel
suggested a walk around the ramparts. The path was broad
enough for Gerald, Darryl, and Richard to join him and walk
abreast.

"Did you know," asked Nigel, "that Lucca was a silk manufacturing center in the eleventh century? Now the money-maker is olive oil. They produce a high quality around here."

"You're a businessman, Richard," said Gerald. "How about setting yourself up here in one of those sixteenth-century palazzos? You could buy one of those food shops by the old amphitheater and live the good life. Good food and wine, terrific weather, maybe an Italian girlfriend or two."

"Great idea, but I'd have to learn Italian," said Richard. "In any case, running your own business isn't all it's cracked up to be. In fact, it's more like a roller coaster ride than anything else. You can spend more time down than up. I'm glad I'm out of it!"

"What business were you in?" asked Nigel, ever curious.

"We converted and distributed specialized paper. I started the company in the late sixties and sold it a couple of years ago. I'll tell you what happened, if you're interested."

The ramparts were broad and leafy, and few people were out in the heat of the day.

"I have a degree in inorganic chemistry and developed some new techniques. One was for coating paper for architects and engineers who needed multiple copies of large drawings."

"You mean like blueprints?" asked Darryl.

"Yes, but a more sophisticated version. You apply yellow chemicals to paper or polyester film onto which you want to copy a drawing. When you put the architectural drawing on top of this coated paper and expose it to bright light, the light bleaches out everything except where the lines of the drawing are. Then you expose the paper to ammonia, and the lines themselves turn black. Of course, I'm simplifying the process. You need a big machine with glass drums for the copying.

"Anyway, that was the core part of the business. Later we became the national distributor for specialist paper manufacturers in other parts of the world. We bought in huge reels of paper, converted them and sold the stuff for industrial use and specialist applications."

"Was that successful?" asked Nigel.

"Yes, it was," said Richard. "In fact, by the early nineteen eighties we were running out of space, and I decided to move the business to a larger and more modern factory. That's where the story comes in.

"Our original factory was built on a large concrete slab on the site of an old marsh. The subsoil was soft and spongy when the floor was laid. But over time, the subsoil dried up, stressing the factory foundations. There were hairline cracks all over the floor, although with machinery and materials lying around I never noticed them. I did notice one thing, though. We used sump pumps to transfer waste into containers, which were then taken away for processing. But you could still see a thin layer of liquid residue on the floor on a Friday evening. It was gone by the following Monday. I remember asking the works' manager about it several times.

"'Don't worry about it,' he said. 'It's taken care of.'

"I was busy at the time, and I put it out of my mind. Until it came time to sell. Before you can sell an industrial site, the quality of the soil has to be checked. The cleaning up of a site like that can be an expensive business, and an inspector was sent out to do some spot-checking, including drilling for soil samples under the concrete floor.

"The inspector broke the news to me and the works' manager in my office. I was stunned. It seems those hairline cracks in the concrete floor had allowed a substantial amount of waste to seep into the soil below. This was highly toxic waste.

"'It's likely to be a nasty mess,' he told us. 'We can't establish the full extent of it until demolition, but you could be talking thousands of pounds to clear it up.'

"For a small business like ours, the financial implications of a full cleanup by an official contractor were not worth thinking about. I was furious with the works' manager for allowing this to happen and he knew it. But fortunately the inspector turned out to be a member of his Masonic lodge.

"'You fellows work it out,' I said, with a pointedly hard edge in my voice. Well, the works' manager took the inspector to lunch and what happened is between them. Not that I approve of using influence or whatever you want to call it, but with the expense of the move. . . .

"I normally pride myself on my business ethics. I've always proceeded on the basis of a handshake and a gentleman's agreement. And I've always been scrupulous about repaying favors. You never know when you might need to call on people. Of course, in this case the works' manager knew he owed me one. He had been responsible for waste disposal and he knew I could have fired him on the spot without benefits or pension.

"After we abandoned the site and demolished the factory, we removed the toxic soil ourselves. The works' manager arranged it with a cheap-and-dirty local company he knew. There was no one else around at the time, and the two of us agreed to keep the matter confidential. We informed the purchasers that all contaminated soil had been removed. They were focusing on the design of a modest residential housing complex for the site and seemed satisfied.

"So I survived that crisis. But a new one loomed several years later. They started to introduce plain paper machines capable of copying large format plans. Draftsmen would no longer need the more elaborate copying process using coated paper. There was no way we could compete with this development; the disappearance of our market was just a matter of time. I felt sick with worry. Living, breathing, and dreaming business was what I'd done all my life. In fact, it was being a workaholic that broke up my marriage. We never had kids, which I suppose was a blessing. Anyway, the stress was enormous and I needed some time off.

"Fortunately, I had started seeing Jill, a single mother employed three days a week in the accounts department. I noticed her soon after she was hired. She was a vivacious blonde with the whitest teeth you've ever seen. Most of the male staff, as well as customers, made sure to pass by her desk, chat her up and enjoy that carefree smile. We flirted for several months, but I wasn't sure whether her response was genuine or due to the fact that I was the boss.

"I remember our first date. I was planning to visit a supplier on the South Coast and would be passing near Jill's house. So I told her, casually. 'I'm always in on a Friday lunchtime,' she replied. 'Buy you a drink at the pub,' I said.

"I found the house and knocked on the door. 'Come in,' said Jill, in a short flowered dress that hugged the right places with no visible support. She wound her arms round my neck. Stunned and grateful, I nipped out and bought some paté and champagne, which we consumed naked in bed that afternoon.

"The relationship suited me. Jill was geographically inconvenient, but that had its advantages. We were able to avoid prying eyes and company gossip. During office hours we were scrupulously correct. She did not report to me and I made certain I had no direct contact with her. When I passed her desk, I smiled but never lingered. I don't much believe in office romances, to tell the truth, especially between bosses and employees. They seldom turn out happily.

"But Jill was discreet and she kept me sane. She listened for hours to my business problems and gave me thoughtful advice. As the company's situation deteriorated, however, things became tense. I was seeing Jill twice a week but not making much of an effort, preoccupied as I was with price wars, severance pay, and feelings of impending doom. Also, let's face it, the initial buzz had faded. The dressed-to-kill look at the front door had given way to slacks, and our champagne and paté celebrations had vanished, replaced by beer and shepherd's pie.

"And then there was the little girl. The day of my first visit, Jill had cleverly arranged for her to stay with a friend after school. Since then, her daughter was often around, and that can put a damper on any romance. Not that I wasn't fond of her; we played rough and tumble games. But I enjoyed her in small doses. Maybe it would have been easier if Jill had had a boy. You have to be so careful nowadays. You can be having quite innocent fun with a little girl and be accused of the most dreadful things. I suppose I never felt quite relaxed with her.

"Anyway, as the company's margins on coated paper inched down, we went into defensive mode, working twenty-four/ seven as they say these days, desperately trying to hang onto a share of a declining market. I hired a series of consultants, mostly full of hot air. They talked 'product development' and 'market opportunity,' but had little practical advice. How could a small company such as ours suddenly expect to morph itself into a supplier of computers or computer services?

"I ended up relying on my own instincts. I obviously tried to increase sales of specialist paper imports as the coated paper business declined. I replaced the salesmen, sold the trucks, and subcontracted deliveries. I reduced the staff, firing people I had known twenty years. 'Let go,' they say, and I did. As if I were keeping these decent, hardworking people against their will! How would they live? At some point the number of people 'let go' exceeded the number still employed. At what price should survival be pursued?

"It was these circumstances that led me to decide to bow out. I felt tired and I'd run out of ideas. I knew I could probably sell the company to a competitor, but I was concerned about the staff. I came up with the idea of selling it to Bill and Nick, my two senior managers. They were experienced, younger than me, and energetic. But neither of them had two brass kopecks to rub together.

"Bill was the sales manager, smart, funny and not afraid of getting his hands dirty, loading the vans or assembling orders.

You have to do these things in small companies. People don't realize. It's another world.

"Nick was a newcomer. He was a chartered accountant, a tall, good-looking fellow, oozing self-confidence. He seemed relaxed and unflappable. Maybe this man could steer the company into calmer waters?

"Well, Bill and Nick were delighted at the idea of buying the company and we struck a deal. I would lend them the money to buy me out at an advantageous interest rate, and they would become the joint owners. As part of the agreement, I would retain a number of 'golden shares' that could trump their shares and allow me to step back in, should they default. They were to send me monthly management accounts, and my loan to them would be repaid as a lump sum at the end of three years. This was their proposal. I agreed, but didn't believe the bit about being repaid in three years.

"And so it was. The papers were signed, a watershed moment. With money, however ephemeral, in my pocket and free of day-to-day worry, I could turn my thoughts to my personal life. Should I throw in my lot with Jill? I knew she was deeply invested in our relationship and expected it to lead somewhere. I thought about it, but couldn't make up my mind. Her house was small, certainly too small for me and my things. We'd have to buy a new, bigger house together. To be honest, the status quo suited me. I avoided the subject and put it on my 'too difficult' pile.

"Everything seemed to be moving in the right direction. The company was sold to the staff and I was kept on as a consultant in sales. Things with Jill continued as before. I saw her several times a week. She managed to be free to see me despite her obligations as a single mother. Yet life is never that simple. The management accounts from the new owners were arriving late and, after six months, failed to appear at all.

"'How do you know if you're making a profit?' I asked.

"The fact was, they had me over a barrel. If things went wrong I could exercise my 'golden shares' option, but that meant returning to the life I was trying to avoid. I continued to vent my frustration with Jill, until one evening, as I stroked her back in bed, I sensed a cold shoulder. I vowed to cut out the business talk and just relax while we were together. Jill had to work with these people three days a week.

"Then Bill and Nick announced that repayment in three years would be impractical. Could I extend it to five?

"'What are your assumptions over the five years?' I asked. 'Do you have a cash flow forecast? If so, I haven't seen it.' But in the end I gave in.

"Shortly after that I noticed that Jill had begun to act differently. Some evenings when I wanted to see her she claimed to be busy. I thought she was just playing games, the way women do sometimes. Playing hard to get. But maybe she was worried, depressed. After all, her job was on the line, too.

"And then the economy turned. Profit margins started to fall again and the price war, the acid that eats away at the humor, goodwill, and even honesty of the businessman in a declining market, resumed. *Forget five years,* I thought, *I'll be lucky to get half the capital in ten.* I tried to stay philosophical.

Nick tried to persuade me to lower the interest rate on the loan, but I stood firm: 'No, we have an agreement. Rates go up and down, take the rough with the smooth.'

"This minor victory gave me a heady feeling, and I decided to take a short vacation. The chunnel had just opened, and the idea of a train trip to Paris was exciting. I got a ten-day travel package from London and stayed in a little hotel on the left bank. I did it all: the wine bars, the cafés, the museums, the tour of the Île de la Cité, and the walks along the Seine. I felt free from the yoke of business for the first time in years, and a sense of renewal.

"Next month no interest was paid at all! An oversight, Nick claimed, but I knew it wasn't. The monthly standing order had not been honored. I realized that this was deliberate.

"Meanwhile, I was seeing even less of Jill. My trip to Paris seemed to provoke no envy, and that was a surprise. Maybe she was sick and tired of hearing about the company. She knew well that my irritation was directed at Nick, not her, but I could feel her stiffen as I wrapped my arms around her and teasingly complained about the accounts. Anyway, we had an argument and after that she just said she wanted to think about things for a while. Clearly something was wrong, but I was too preoccupied with getting my money back from the company to focus on our relationship. So I went back to Nick and Bill.

"'Obviously you have a problem. Let's talk about it. What about raising money elsewhere?' I queried hopefully.

"'Not a chance,' said Nick. 'No collateral. Anyway, I've tried that already.' We talked about pricing and discounts.

"'Staff?' I queried. A leaden silence ensued, then the news that they had recently made three people redundant. I was surprised Jill hadn't called me about this. In any case, it looked grim. I gave in yet again, reduced the interest rate two points, and gave them a moratorium on debt repayment until things got better. 'Six months seem reasonable? But for God's sake, give me the monthly figures!'

"Amity restored, I once again shrank from the thought of returning to the company, and to the sullen stares of the staff.

"Despite our agreement, things did not improve. Interest payments, even at the new rate, were few and far between. I tried to keep my cool and take comfort in life's little routines. But it wasn't easy.

"I was missing Jill, so I gave her a call. All of a sudden she was available again. I asked her over and found her more attractive than ever. Or maybe it was those few extra pounds she'd taken off. In any case, it was like old times. I tried to avoid mixing business with pleasure and bought Jill a gold watch for her birthday. I took them both, Jill and her daughter, to Eurodisney in Paris. It was a great success. I quite enjoyed it.

"Then, nine months ago Bill gave me a call. He sounded conspiratorial, speaking in a low voice. What did I think of the offer from Worldwide Graphics? I was baffled. I asked what he was talking about and heard the silence of embarrassment. Had they been negotiating a takeover without the courtesy of telling me?

"'Nick was supposed to call you.'

"'Was he? Well, he didn't.' I replied.

"'Oh, hell. Worldwide Graphics approached Nick six months ago. They want to create one big manufacturer/wholesaler for specialized paper and drafting materials, to have more clout with retailers. Seems a good idea.' I agreed.

"'First they made a silly offer and Nick turned them down. Then they came back with better terms. He's turned them down again.'

"'Without your approval?'

"'Look, I'm the technical guy. He's in charge of finance.'

"If Bill sees it like that, it's his problem, I thought. But how could Nick turn down an offer without consulting me? I was furious. His first duty should be to the shareholders and suppliers of capital.

"'Bill,' I said, 'let me ask you something. Do you want to be taken over? It may mean giving up the job of company director. It may even mean a lower salary, smaller car, who knows? You've been working flat out to keep the company going. What do *you* want?'

"'Quite honestly,' he replied, 'titles and cars don't bother me, but the pension does. They say they'll guarantee that. And they say they'll also pay you out. Nick's new to the company. He can't understand loyalty. To him you're just the money guy. But I want to see your loan repaid.'

"'What do you want from me?'

"'I want you to talk to Worldwide. I am not an accountant. They'd run rings round me. I'll ask them to contact you. But let's keep this conversation quiet, can we?'

"The boss of Worldwide turned out to be a straight talking man. He said, 'Those fellows haven't a clue! The accounts! What a mess!'

"'They owe me a lot of money.'

"'I know. I'm doing the best I can for everyone. Pay back your debt, keep the good staff, keep the name going, all that.' Keep the name going? He hooked me with that one.

"The truth quickly came out, the truth about the irrecoverable loan made by Nick to an insolvent local retailer, and the truth about the overvalued inventory. Then I got the kicker. Worldwide not only wanted Nick out, they wanted me to pay for his redundancy.

"'Steady on,' I said. 'I'm just a creditor. Would you charge the Hong Kong and Shanghai Bank for your redundancies? That's your problem.'

"'Not so,' came the answer.

"I raised my right to exercise the golden shares and take back effective control.

"'Do by all means,' he said politely. He had called my bluff and I agreed to cooperate.

"I met with Bill and Nick in the conference room at company head office and pretended that all three of us knew the history of the takeover offer. I didn't ask why the company had been negotiating without my knowledge. No recriminations or reference to delayed loan payments, monthly reports and so on. Worldwide had contacted me directly and I now believed the revised terms should be accepted.

"Like a thunderclap, Nick exploded across the table.

"'How the hell did you get involved in this?'

"'Worldwide phoned me.'

"'You've no right to interfere. We were at a crucial stage in the negotiations.'

"'Not according to Worldwide. You turned them down twice.'

"'I've got my own negotiating strategy. We're the owners of this company now, not you,' he snarled across the table. 'Keep your bloody hands out of our business!'

"'I have here an agreement, signed by you,' I said. 'Look at page eighteen. It's the sale and loan agreement you signed three years ago. I've marked the clauses you've broken in red pencil. You can see I could legally invoke my golden shares.'

"'You agreed to every change we made.'

"'Verbally, not in writing. Under duress, not willingly.' I changed my tone, more conciliatory. 'Look Nick, the wise skipper knows when to get the crew into the lifeboats.'

"'You know nothing about this negotiation and you're terrified of losing your bloody money!'

"'It's too late, Nick. The wagons have circled and you're on the outside.' And then Nick put his ace of spades on the table.

"'Take a look at this,' he said and handed me an invoice dated fifteen years earlier. Yes, it was the invoice from the cheap-and-dirty company we had hired to clean up our industrial waste.

"'I'm sure the directors of Worldwide would be interested in that,' Nick said with a smirk, gesturing at the piece of paper in my hand. 'They're unlikely to purchase a company with a potential lawsuit. I wonder if the people living on the company's old site have been suffering from headaches or gastro-intestinal problems? How do we know there aren't a lot of nasty chemicals left in the soil?'

"*Blackmail,* I thought! Why indeed would Worldwide want to inherit a potential court case?"

"You could have faced punitive damages, you realize that," said Nigel, clearly alarmed.

"I imagined myself appearing before a judge as the prosecutor pressed his case: 'The soil on your old factory site shows high levels of diazo chemical residues, chemicals which among other things are used for the manufacture of (and here he would turn to the Court with emphasis) explosives. Where is the certification for the cleanup of the site?'"

"Explosives? Is that true?" asked Darryl.

"We weren't making explosives ourselves, but that's what the chemicals were originally designed for, in Germany."

"It's just as well you're telling us this in confidence," remarked Nigel.

"I know you don't want to do me in, Nigel, but Nick did! I said as much to Jill that night as she slipped a leg comfortably between my own, as she usually did before we nodded off.

"'The takeover's a good deal. It could mean a promotion for you. Now it looks like a dead duck.'

"'But why?' she asked.

"'Nick's holding something over my head, something that never should have happened, something I hoped was dead but could be very much alive.'

"'What is it?' she replied, and I told her the story of the waste chemicals and how we had saved money by trying a do-it-yourself cleanup job. I didn't fill in all the details, just said that Nick had found out about it.

"'Richard, can I tell you something?' Jill sat up in bed, smoothing the bedclothes neatly around her. 'You know how much Nick resents you? With that loan of yours, you're still the effective owner of the business. Well, Nick started flirting with me. He must have known about our relationship. It was a way of getting at you. At first it seemed casual, and innocent. But as your confrontations with him escalated, so did Nick's overtures to me.'

"So the lazy sonofabitch was busy seducing Jill instead of preparing the accounts, I thought to myself.

"'I was frustrated at the time, I couldn't get through to you,' she said. 'You were obsessed and touchy. I'd say eruptive. You thought we had a relationship, but I saw it going nowhere. I felt you were taking me for granted. We'd sit for hours talking about the company. I knew Nick was selfish, but, like it or not, he's attractive and charming when he wants to be. He took me to a couple of West End restaurants, and to a play.'

"My imagination was in overload. I knew she'd gone to bed with him. *What did he do? How much did she like it?* I had trouble concentrating on what she was saying.

"'Well, I knew it wouldn't last, but I enjoyed the attention. And then he dropped me abruptly. No excuse, not even a kind word. Just on to the next woman.'

"So that's why you became available again, I thought, and Jill continued, 'One evening, quite recently, I ran into Nick, outside the local pub. "Come have a drink, Jill," he said. I was cool, I can tell you, but my curiosity got the better of me, and,

well, he's damned attractive. Despite my best intentions, we ended up back at his place.'

"'We had a more-than-usual selfish encounter. I felt used in a way I had never felt before. Then he told me about the offer for the company. I asked whether he had spoken to you about it and he laughed and said "Screw Richard!" I tried to talk to him, but he turned his back on me and went to sleep. I lay there for a while and vowed I would somehow get back at him. I dressed and left before he woke up. Now's my chance.'

"'You have something on him?' I sat up, more attentive now.

"Jill told me that, working in the accounts department, she had documented proof that Nick had not only been using his AMEX card for private purposes, he had recently been transferring company money into the private account of a Margaret Walker. She had quietly established that Ms. Walker was neither an employee nor a supplier. The amounts were large, and blowing the whistle on him could prevent him ever getting another job as a Chartered Accountant, let alone a company director.

"'Jill, I love you!' The moment I said the words I regretted them. Lovely girl, Jill, but you know. . . .

"'Do you, Richard, really? I hope so, I really do,' she said."

"And did you trump Nick's ace of spades?" asked Gerald.

"Did I ever! The sale went through. Nick was made redundant, my money's in the bank, and I recovered the dreaded invoice. And here I am on holiday, agonizing."

"Agonizing? Shouldn't you be celebrating!" asked Darryl.

"Well, as she saw me off at Heathrow, Jill kissed me and said, 'Richard, sweetheart, I wish I were coming with you.

Maybe next time. I must say, I can't blame you; you need a break. It was all such a sordid business.'

"She paused, then said, 'Wouldn't it be terrible if the people who live on the old factory site claimed they were getting sick from those horrible chemicals you told me about?'

"'It certainly would!' I said, appalled, and then thought: *She had the same access to old invoices that Nick had had. Surely, she wouldn't . . . ?*

"'Oh, darling,' she said. "I saw a lovely house down in Reigate yesterday. You'll love it. Shall we go to see it when you get back?'

"I left her looking glowing and expectant. She was wearing the same short, flowered dress she had worn when I first stopped by her house years before. It clung to her figure in the same way and had the same effect on me. And yet. . . ."

There was a pause as the four men continued their walk around the ramparts, gazing over Lucca's ancient streets and campaniles. Richard furrowed his brow.

"I wonder how long it takes to learn Italian?"

‒ The Divorcée's Tale ‒

Lizzie

Here's a woman, fresh from two divorces,
Who barely draws a breath as she discourses.
Nervous and wide-eyed, hollow-cheeked but tanned,
Relaxed, although her status is *un-manned*.
Her eyebrows plucked and highlights in her hair,
Heels somewhat high and nails beyond compare,
A knitted top and smartly fitting slacks,
No cook is she but lives on bought-in snacks.
She has uncomplicated, simple views,
Prefers to watch a soap and not the news.
With all such make-believe she is bewitched,
And knows who will get pregnant or get hitched.
Romantic, she is trusting and naïve,
She wears her open heart upon her sleeve.
Men catch their breath on glimpsing breast or thigh
But, truth be known, her IQ's not that high.

We approached San Gimignano from the north through vine-yards and fields of wild oats, their silvery heads shining in the sun. The fifteen remaining towers of the town looked closer than they were. We entered by La Rocca, a fourteenth-century Florentine fortress on the highest bit of ground, and exited on the far side, to the south. We passed by more vine-yards, a quail park, and an old watermill, before arriving in late afternoon at a small hotel adjoining a tenth-century monastery.

For dinner we were given a medieval pilgrim's meal of bread soaked in broth followed by vegetable stew and tasteless bean mash. Fortunately, an excellent wine was served as an accompaniment. After dinner, we moved out onto the terrace where we sat for a while sipping limoncello. The following day was an optional hike, so there was less incentive than usual to retire on the early side.

Richard turned to Lizzie, whom he found attractive. Getting her to talk would give him legitimate reason to keep her in view without being too obvious.

"What brings you on a trip like this?" he asked. "I'm surprised those politicians in Washington let you out of their sight."

"You'd be surprised how few are eligible."

"So how do you spend your time?" asked Gerald, giving Richard a bit of support.

"Oh, I work part time answering phones for a consulting firm. I'm supposed to 'decorate' the front office. Sometimes I run out to Starbucks for a coffee or do some filing. Mindless, I know, but I don't want a demanding job. I've enough to do at home. Five bedrooms and a living room the size of a pool hall. You see, I'm from the south. Starting at ten suits me fine."

"Doesn't sound too taxing," Richard agreed. "But you haven't explained the trip." The rest of us moved closer.

"Okay, I'll start from the beginning. Maureen—she's my friend—Maureen and I meet for lunch on Tuesdays and swap stories, gossip really. I generally bitch about Fearson. That's my ex. It was Fearson who left behind the SUV. That was all he did leave behind. He had to have a big sports utility vehicle, of course. Had to keep up. To the tune of thirty-five thousand dollars! I hated driving the damn thing, but at least I got something from him. Of course, I got to keep the house, too.

"Maureen was always there for me while it was going on. The breakup, that is. Mind you, she never did like Fearson, but then no one did. Easily irritated, never content. One of those 'number one' characters they talk about in enneagrams. I wish I'd known about enneagrams before I married him. It's too late for that now. Nothing was ever good enough, quick enough, or professional enough for Fearson.

"I miss him in a way. Not the company! He was always ranting and raving about the Republicans and guns and how the rich are getting richer. In the end I just said 'yes, dear' and tuned him out. Next thing I knew he had an earnest young liberal lawyer in tow, hanging onto his every word. Well, she's welcome to him. It's more not having anyone around to figure things out for me.

"Anyway, both kids are gone now and I thought it was time I tried something new. I had that restless feeling, you know. It was my son, Parker, who got me interested in computers. Well, it's natural, with him working in Silicon Valley and all. He was back home for Thanksgiving with Sun Ying. Nice girl, very polite, with one of those envy-making figures they tend to have. The two of them talked computers nonstop. *Uh-oh*, I thought, *obsessive, like his father.* But they did a selling job on me, no doubt about that. First thing I knew, I'd bought a computer.

"Tell the truth, I felt a bit resentful, like I'd been forced into it. But they did have a point. E-mail's the thing to keep in touch. 'You can't, like, not have it, Mom.' So that's how I got started.

"I wasted time learning the hard way how to set up the address book and then go to 'tools' and 'recipients' to avoid typing in Parker's address every time I sent him a message. It would have been easier just to type it in. But I felt more confident once I caught on to AOL. AOL is what they call an IVP. ISP? Something like that. Anyway, there was a very nice young man there, calm and patient, I thought. He talked me through what I needed to know. Later I bought a yellow and black book called *E-mail for Dummies,* but it didn't cover any of my problems.

"I managed to get going, but it was rough. I'd be right in the middle of a message when it would disappear and turn up in 'drafts.' Overrated, these machines. But never give up, that's what I say. I wasn't going to be licked by the stupid thing. If you don't join in, you're sort of left behind. So I started experimenting, surfing the web, typing in my favorite companies to see if they had any new products.

"Well, one day I found this site called 'popular chats,' and under it 'romance.' So I clicked on both. It asked me for my age. Over eighteen, I typed in. There were these internet cafés. I chose 'Love Café,' feeling sort of daring. My heart rate went up two points. Then they wanted a nickname. More difficult.

I called myself Needinlove and clicked 'go.' *This is ridiculous,* I thought, but it was only six o'clock and too early for dinner.

"Well there were dozens of people with equally silly names joining and leaving this chat room, people like K-dogg and Javaqueen. The conversation went something like this:

DawnB: *Hello room.*
Computer: *DawnB has left the room.*
Root Beer: *Yes, hello room.*
Twix: *Hello room. I'm 23/m/OR.*
Computer: *Twix has left the conversation.*
M.CarmelBear: *How is everyone.*
Computer: *Grizz has joined the conversation.*
Grizz: *Hey ladies, what are u doing today. Hi, Love Honey.*
Computer: *Love Honey has left the conversation.*
Winner: *Is anyone from WI? Perhaps people will take notice of me now. Duh.*
Pumper boy: *Hotnhunky is known as most wanted.*
Hysteria: *Funny face.*
Computer: *Buns25 has left the conversation.*

"People have time for this? I sent a whisper message to Grizz, who asked if anyone had anything intelligent to say. He said he was forty, male, and an executive with The Gap. He asked for my profile and I was tempted to say that I have a large nose. But I didn't. I played it straight and it soon turned out that Grizz was fourteen and was having fun with her classmates. At my expense. I don't mind being asked if I want to be on the bottom or the top, but I'd like to be asked by someone who knows what it means. I was glad my son couldn't see me.

"I went back to the chat room and before too long I had a whisper message from BigMike. I'd noticed some comments from him, more intelligible than most. After the teenspeak, like, I needed an ordinary conversation. So I sent my own whisper message to BigMike. He said he was 29/m/VA, but I knew he might be older than that. Men lie about their age as much as women. But if he wasn't twenty-nine, well at least he could spell. So I said I was 35/f/MD. You could be talking to anyone, you know! Wouldn't it be embarrassing if it turned out to be Maureen's daughter Kelsey, or someone else I knew?

"He started by asking if I'd like a sensible conversation.

"I replied, 'What do you mean?'

"He said, 'We could use plain English for a start.'

"I said, 'All right, that suits me fine.'

"He said, 'I like living in the country, dressing casual, having my own space. But the people around here are as dumb as they come.'

"'Then you've got yourself a dilemma, haven't you?' I replied. 'Do you go onto these chat lines much?'

"'Sure. It gives me a feeling of company,' he said, 'even if the person I'm chatting with is in Australia. It gets lonely in rural Virginia.'

"Then I said it was time for dinner, and what I was having, and he said he was a night owl and it was too soon for dinner.

"He said, 'Fortunately you're not in Australia. Only Maryland. Let's meet back here tomorrow, same time.'

"I had a feeling of achievement. It was easy being open with someone you'd never see face to face. But that night I lay awake wondering about BigMike. What did he do in rural Virginia? As I drifted in and out of sleep, I imagined an Appalachian lumberjack striding up the driveway, hunting rifle in hand, a bandanna around his neck. I wasn't made for the single life.

"I went on line again the following day. It was raining, I remember, not a day to put the petunias in. I like to keep up appearances, but the petunias could wait.

"'I've got a gun,' he says. 'You have to have one these days.'

"'Is it dangerous down there?' I asked.

"'No, not in this part of Virginia, but everyone has one. I do target practice on crows,' he said, 'thirty yards away, maybe more. It keeps up my skills.'

"Turns out he was overseas in the Air Force for a while. Then he quit and did some selling. Now he makes his living as a writer.

"'What do you write?' I asked.

"'Training manuals.' *Training manuals? In rural Virginia?*

"'So you're technical,' I typed.

"'Guess so.'

"'Maybe you can help me. I've got this new vehicle, only three thousand miles on it. I'm wondering when the first service's due.'

"'Depends,' he said. 'Did you read the manual?'

"Now I used to leave that to my ex-husband, but I realized just in time that to mention my ex-husband might sound as if I were advertising I was single. Also, I hadn't a clue where the manual was, so I just typed 'No.'

"'New cars are better than they used to be,' he told me. 'I remember when you had to service them after five hundred miles.' Well, the guy definitely wasn't twenty-nine. Gave himself away there. 'Nowadays could be five, seven thousand. As I say, it depends. What is it, what model?' I told him.

"'Nice,' he said. 'Find the manual, or phone the dealer. I'd better not guess.' *Fair enough,* I thought. I was just being lazy. I have to get used to thinking of these things myself.

"'Got any kids?' I asked.

"'Two, but they're with my ex-wife in Georgia.'

"'Oh,' I said. 'Boys?'

"'Both models,' he replied.

"'Are they in school?' I asked.

"'Yep, the girl goes locally in Atlanta. The boy's in Pennsylvania.'

"'How come?'

"'Penn State.' He'd blown that one. *No way was he twenty-nine years old!*

"'I see,' I said, 'you must have been a precocious nine year old if you have a son in college. You're never twenty-nine.'

"'No, I lied to you.'

"'Why'd you do that?'

"'Why not?'

"'Meaning?'

"'Never mind. You got me and I'm forty-eight.'

"'I'm forty-six.'

"Over the next few days, he told me how he'd found his wife packing to leave. She hated rural Virginia and wanted to live in a big city. I heard about his divorce, and I told him about Parker and Brenda and then about Fearson and the part-time job, and what I liked for breakfast. By and by he asked me whether I have any special friends and what we do together. 'Not prying,' he said. But I've got nothing to hide, so there was no reason to get annoyed.

"Then I went off on vacation. Maureen and I had planned it for months. A cruise, you know, the Caribbean. Organized deck games, loud shirts and post-prostate, middle-aged men with bullhorn ties and wives called Mildred who wore dark glasses that turned up at the corners and asked why St. Maartin has two a's. It was a nice break, but I was glad to get home at the end of it.

"There were several e-mails waiting for me, one from Microsoft pushing some new games software and another from a company wanting me to download their gear to listen to the latest dance music. Never thought I'd be leaping at the computer to retrieve e-mails within minutes of returning home.

"Yes, there were two e-mails from BigMike, one hoping I'd had a good vacation, and would I tell him about it. The other, dated three days later, announced that he was coming to Washington on business, and could we meet. It seems the Pentagon needed some updating of old technical manuals on some of the standard aircraft and they were looking for some low-cost outsourcing. *Nice to know they're so cost conscious,* I thought. He said if he got the contract, he would have work for a year or more and might possibly move to D.C. Perhaps we could celebrate together?

"I felt conflicted. On the one hand our e-relationship had evolved and he seemed like a decent, regular guy. On the other I didn't know his real name, he didn't know mine, and common sense told me to keep it that way. You hear stories about internet dating. But what's so wrong with a meeting? *Keep it in a public place,* I thought, *nothing more, see what happens.* In any case I'm a tad adventurous at heart and this was an adventure.

"I replied, 'Sure, let's celebrate, but you got to get the contract first.'

"So he replies, 'We can still celebrate, it doesn't need an excuse.'

"Funny, that. Completely different from Fearson. I can't remember us celebrating anything. Well, be fair, we did on our wedding, when we went to a small hotel in the Northern Neck. The hotel had Virginia wine, I remember, and the waitress had nothing to do and talked to us through dinner. The sex was great, really great. But Fearson wore himself out and three days later he was back to work, and so was I. Things trailed off after that.

"Oh hell, I thought, *life's short.* I rang Maureen and told her about BigMike.

"'Invite me to the wedding,' she said.

"'You gotta be joking,' I replied.

"'Seriously though, you be careful, Lizzie. You know nothing about him, really. Can you check him out?'

"'You mean get a Dun & Bradstreet on him?' I asked. 'That's not going to tell me if he's into chains and leather.'

"'If he is, let me know,' says Maureen. 'Tell you what I'll do. I'll ask Joan to make some inquiries. You remember, she's my cousin who works at the Pentagon. At least you'll know if he's spinning you a yarn.'

"Meanwhile no harm in just meeting, I thought, but I didn't want to give him my home address. So I suggested we meet at

the Georgetown Starbucks on Wisconsin Avenue, sort of halfway between me and the Pentagon. It's where they had those murders back in 1997, or whenever, although I hadn't thought of that when I suggested it.

"He was spot on time. *Good start,* I thought. I'd say a young forty-eight, hair graying and pushed back at the sides, brown leather jacket, open shirt, suede shoes. A bit arty, if you know what I mean. He peppered me with questions as if I were the most fascinating woman in the world. I guess I was hungry for that sort of thing, for *any* attention, to tell the truth.

"We talked so hard we almost forgot to order, but I did get a latte. Can't remember what he had. I wore some new slacks and a white blouse with a ruffle down the front, the feminine touch. Oh, and a gold necklace with matching earrings. I'd had my hair done the day before, but it was windy that morning and wouldn't stay in place. I thought, *I'll have to find another hairdresser. Arnold doesn't use enough spray and it flies all over the place.*

"When it came time to leave, I realized I had asked him nothing much about himself, except his name, which was Mike, after all. But I admit I enjoyed it. He was a perfect gentleman, no suggestions or come-ons. He was staying, he said, at some hotel in Crystal City, but he didn't ask me to go there. I was waiting for it, but the question never came, and I felt relaxed about it all.

"We had exchanged phone numbers, and two days later Mike called. Would I meet him the next day, same time, same place? I phoned Maureen again.

"'Get him talking about himself,' she said. 'Men love it. The way to a man's heart is through his ego. Other things as well, but start with his ego.' She's always been supportive like that. 'And by the way, I phoned Joan. She said she'd make some inquiries.'

"This time Starbucks was empty. My hair was looking better, I'd used Freeze It on it that morning. I wore some costume jewelry and a braided blue jacket. Maureen told me I sometimes overdid the rouge, so I was careful about the makeup. Once again I found myself answering Mike's questions. Somehow he always managed to bring the subject back to me. But eventually we got around to his work, and he seemed a different person. The relaxed charm faded and he became the tough businessman. Well, a businessman has to be focused and aggressive, and he was probably successful at what he did. He told me how in he was with the Defense people. He had plenty of work, profitable work, he said. His Pentagon contacts had virtually promised him the contract, and he knew a good graphic artist who could do the illustrations.

"By this time I was hooked, I admit it. I felt young and alive again. Don't try too hard, Lizzie, I told myself. He was attractive, and seemed to be a professional. We women like success in a man, although just finding someone with manners is a triumph these days. Yes, I was hooked and the excitement of it pushed any doubts I may have had aside. The main problem, it seemed to me, was that he lived in the middle of nowhere. But then what was so wonderful about Bethesda, Maryland, if it came to that?

"He told me he would let me in on a secret. He was planning to start a magazine specializing in technical maintenance and repair.

"'There's nothin' like it on the market,' he said. 'At least, not the sort of thing I have in mind. I've held it close to my chest 'til now. But everythin's fallin' into place. The Defense contract will pay most of my overheads while I'm gettin' the magazine off the ground.'

"He'd done a business plan.

"'See, here,' he said, and strewed the table with sheets of paper covered with figures and projections. I saw a name, Mike Jenkins, at the corner of one of the pages. Well, Maureen could give her cousin Joan at the Pentagon more to go on.

"This was all way beyond me, but I didn't let on. He even had a mock-up, he called it, of a front cover with the front of an F-something fighter and a mechanic in overalls. The bottom line was, he said, that there would be an eighteen percent return, probably more.

"'The stock market is overvalued,' he said. 'It isn't the time to risk your capital on new stocks.'

"But the magazine was a great opportunity. Technical, you see, nuts and bolts stuff, not some internet flight of fancy. He had already arranged for the legal work, and four other people were putting in money. He was expecting an IPO (whatever that is) in five years, maybe less. It wouldn't be like the tech stocks, but then it wouldn't be as risky either, he repeated. And he rattled on about the market and the opportunities in China where manufacturing had relocated. I was impressed.

"If Mike had told me he had a cure for the common cold, I think I'd have been smart enough to say 'Hey, wait a minute!' I mean, I'm not stupid. I went to a community college and did psychology as part of my sociology degree. I got married before I did the masters. That was my biggest mistake, but I would have been accepted into the program.

"The project sounded practical and mainstream, and he was so enthusiastic. I found myself asking how much each person had to invest, and he said twenty thousand dollars. Was I interested?

"'Could be. But that's a lot of money,' I said, 'I don't just have money lying around in the bank.'

"Mike said, 'I've raised a mortgage on my own house. It's what you do if you believe in a project.'

"Oh, no, I thought, no way, not that, if that's what he's hinting. I had begun to feel awkward, you know. He seemed to pick up on it.

"'Oh, don't get me wrong,' he said, with that smile that said I think you misunderstood me. 'Someone like you, you shouldn't invest the roof over your head. It's different for me, of course. I know the project and I know it'll work. If you're goin' to invest, stick to the blue chip companies. I'm sorry, you must have thought I was shapin' up to hit you for some money,' and he laughed, all natural.

"*So reasonable, so sensible,* I thought. *Even if he's trying me out, I can't blame him for raising money where he can.*

"'It's okay,' I replied. 'I'm interested. It sounds like a good idea.'

"'Let's talk when the company's off the ground and you see the profit comin' in. Less risky that way.'

"'No, seriously, count me in. It would add a bit of excitement to my life.'

"'Look,' he said, 'if you really mean that, maybe you could do a deal with that SUV of yours. You say it's just sittin' in the drive. Hell, you get nine miles to the gallon if you're lucky. And servicin' costs a fortune. They assume you're filthy rich and charge you two arms and a leg.'

"I suspected he was right on this. What I needed was a small compact I could park easily. I didn't have young kids or dozens of bags of groceries to cart around.

"'If you're interested,' he said, 'I'll show it to a friend of mine while I'm here. He's well-heeled and talks about gettin' an SUV. He's got a big family, and they've got this small Honda. It's almost new, isn't it? I mean your SUV. He lives in Arlington. I could see what he'd give you for it. Probably be a pretty good price and you'd have enough left over after the investment to get a good second-hand car. Really. You got the vehicle here?'

"It was difficult to argue, I must say. I knew Fearson had paid thirty-five, but the second hand people would probably give me twenty thousand max. If I could get thirty from Mike's friend, make a good investment, and then get myself a second-hand car like he said, I'd be better off all the way around. I hated that SUV anyway.

"Before I realized what I was doing, I handed over the keys to the car and Mike had gone. I went home on a number 32 bus. Excited though I was, I still didn't want him dropping me off at home. Afterwards I remembered I kept one of the registration cards in the glove compartment.

"Later that evening, I began to get anxious. I called the phone number Mike had given me. His cellphone wasn't switched on. I kept trying. *Why hadn't he called?* The following morning I called the number again. Still no Mike. I phoned Maureen.

"'Maureen, I've got a problem.' I told her about the SUV and about Mike's disappearance. 'No, don't say it. You warned me. I'm real dumb, I know. So what do I do now?'

"'Get the cops onto to it, quick,' she told me. 'They might find it, although I doubt it. And next time, talk to your friend Maureen before trusting any more strange men!'

"Half an hour later a police car swept into my driveway, the yellow light flashing. A policeman jumped out. He was big and muscular, with blonde hair and a trim moustache. With the big belt and the gun, I felt safe and protected. I can't resist a uniform.

"'G'mornin', ma'am. I understand you've lost a vehicle.' Only he pronounced it 've-hi-cle.'

"'Yes, officer, a silver Toyota Landcruiser.'

"'Where didya lose it?' I felt tongue-tied and nervous. He was so tall and his shoulders were broad.

"'I've got some coffee brewing,' I told him. He hesitated.

"'Thank you, ma'am. I don't usually, but. . . .'

"So I told Larry—his name was Larry—how my ex-husband had left me with this SUV, how I'd met Mike on a chat site, his business with the Pentagon, and his offer to sell the car.'

"'Did this Mike tell you who he was taking the car to?'

"'No, just that it was someone in Arlington.'

"'Not much to go on.'

"'He seemed such a nice guy, reliable and polite.'

"'They all do. We're getting a lot of these scams lately,' Larry said, and he sat down at the kitchen table with his coffee and completed his hot sheet.

"'We'll task it out and get back to you.'

"'Do you think he's pocketed the cash and beat town?' I felt such a fool.

"'Likely he took it to a chop shop and had it dismantled. That way it's harder to trace. They'll cannibalize it and sell the parts,' he explained. My heart sank.

"Later, that evening, Larry returned in his squad car. 'Any news from your friend, Mike?' he asked. 'Mmmh, thought not. I guess you've lost the car and the money, ma'am.'

"'Call me Lizzie,' I told him. He'd just come off duty, so I poured him a drink. Soon I was telling him about my divorce and he was telling me about his job, and his vacation in Florida.

"Larry had just asked if we could get together sometime the next week, when a taxi pulled up outside the house. I could see a man in the back hand over the fare to the driver. Out stepped Mike.

"*Oh my God!* I thought. Mike paused and looked at the police car in the drive. I could see him, tight-lipped, glance at the sky. He then came to the house and rang the bell.

"'Hey, what's the story?' said Mike, eyeing Larry, then me.

"'The lady's reported a stolen ve-hi-cle,' said Larry, all official.

"I felt two feet high and wanted to hide under the table. But at that moment the phone rang. It was Maureen.

"'Have I got news for you! Your Mike Jenkins is on the level.' I told her I'd phone her back.

"When I turned around, there was Mike, his hand outstretched, holding an envelope.

"'Here's your Landcruiser,' he said, unsmiling. The check was for twenty-five thousand dollars.

"'Guess you got a good deal,' said Larry, picking up his cap and heading for the door. 'Not bad, second-hand.'

"Mike and I stared at each other for a moment. I was speechless with embarrassment.

"'Mike, I tried to phone you, several times. I thought. . . .'

"'I think I know what you thought,' he replied, stony-faced.

"'Well, what happened? Where have you been?'

"'Lizzie, I do business with folks I trust and with folks who trust me. The check gives the name and address of my friend who bought the car. Send him the title.' And with that he simply walked out of the house."

"Did you ever find out what happened?" asked Richard.

"I phoned the guy who bought the Toyota. His wife had had a suspected stroke while Mike was there. Mike took them to the hospital and stayed with them while they did the tests. Somewhere along the way he lost his cellphone."

"Did you try to contact Mike and patch things up?" asked Moira.

"I sent him several messages, apologizing and offering to send him the cash to invest. But he never replied."

"And the police officer, what happened there?" asked Nicola.

"Married, of course," muttered Lizzie, looking intently at her shoes. "So I decided to blow some of the money, and here I am."

Richard looked at her and shifted in his chair. He wasn't sure whether to dismiss this silly woman, admire her simple honesty, or treat her story as an elaborate come-on. She was rather attractive, though, and hell, they were on holiday. When they were both out of earshot of the other walkers, Richard said to Lizzie:

"I think I'll go into Siena tomorrow. Like to come along?"

━ The Bureaucrat's Tale ━

Shirley

A senior civil servant, valued highly,
A lady, stern in face, in spirit wily,
To migraine headaches clearly is she prone;
She has a cat, but lives elsewise alone.
Thin-lipped she is, of humor quite devoid;
A dinner partner one can well avoid.
Yet behind the homely face does lurk
A brain as sharp as mustard when at work.
Her rivals in a memo she'll demolish
And paraphrase a policy with polish.
Issues are seen by some as black or white,
You're judged entirely wrong or wholly right.
Our Shirley, who resists naïveté,
Sees policy in subtle shades of gray.
But be not fooled, while she will give and take,
This is no lenient enemy to make.

We left the monastery behind us and walked past the famous towns of Pienza, Montepulciano, and Montalcino, all seen in the distance. For a while, we followed a track parallel to the old Via Cassia, until we reached the watershed by the Fortress of Radicofani. We crossed a meadow full of variegated black and white butterflies, and another, vivid yellow, with its bushes of gorse.

Soon we were entering a volcanic area, with rich soil and lakes, that attracted some of the first Etruscan settlements. But the area also included the Bardone Valley. Dry and treeless, the Bardone Valley was the most bleak and desolate place on our walk. We strode grimly down the path until Jeremy stopped at an unexpected dewpond. Shirley, Moira, and Randall joined him and together they watched hundreds of small green frogs jumping into the water.

"I wouldn't mind a rest," said Moira, wiping her neck and forehead with a paisley cloth.

Her companions sat on the ground beside her and searched their backpacks for water.

"I think it's your turn to tell us a tale, Shirley," said Randall.

"I don't think I could match your stories. My life is dull in comparison. I don't travel or go to fancy parties."

"Then tell us something about your work," said Moira.

"I've always been reluctant to talk about my job," said Shirley wryly. "The Federal Government isn't popular in some quarters, as you know, and isn't respected in others."

"It's a closed book to me. I'm sure a lot of people wonder about it," said Randall.

"How do you find it, yourself?" asked Moira.

"Personally, a government job suits me. I'm a self-starter. I like structure and clear procedures, and I like being efficient. For example, I cut out all my junk mail, just cut it off at the source. And I never pick up the same piece of paper twice. I read it and then assign it, file it, or throw it away. A good bureaucrat has to be able to skim, to have an eye for the useful fact, and to be able to tease it out of a long article. These are standard skills. Most of us develop them, and then you add in a few of your own tricks. I always work in the morning when I'm most productive, and I return phone calls and hold my meetings in the afternoon. I learned early on to write short memos—crisp and to the point. My superiors appreciate the brevity. They don't want to bother with the fine points."

"Let's have it, Shirley," said Jeremy. "I suspect there's a story in there somewhere."

"All right," said Shirley. "I know some people imagine government as a bland, slow-paced bureaucracy, but it can also be a dog eat dog world! Especially for someone who's mid-career.

"Some years ago I was working for the Department of Overseas Investment. We were located in a typical government office building, with pale green walls and linoleum floors. The DOI brought together the interests of Treasury, Commerce, and the State Department.

"I was single, so I had flexibility in my daily schedule. I could please my superiors by arriving at seven in the morning to produce drafts of correspondence assigned to me at a COB meeting the evening before. (Oh, that's 'close of business' meeting.) And I could dismay my subordinates by staying late in the evening to supervise the finalization of the weekly cable to the field.

"Well, I had been in the department about two years with the job of 'senior advisor' when our director was promoted out and we got a new director."

"What was he like?" asked Randall, interested to see how mid-level employees judged their superiors.

"I'll get to that. Let's just say for now that Donald had dark wavy hair, a determined thrust of the jaw and a firm, impersonal regard. Rather good looking, except that he was fat. Anyway, he arrived in the department at ten A.M. one Wednesday morning, and by Friday he had drawn up a new office layout and a modified chain of command. A new office configuration was a status symbol for incoming directors. In Donald's case, it was achieved by tearing down and remounting several partitions and putting the secretaries in a pool rather than leaving them near the officers they served. He also managed to locate a black leather couch for his office.

"Donald said he planned to keep me on as his senior advisor and wanted to rely on me for substantive advice. I'm good at policy analysis, so I looked forward to the challenge. However, the special briefing papers he requested were in addition to my primary job of reviewing the departmental work plus the reports of our colleagues in related departments. I knew I'd be stretched, but I agreed to stay on in good faith. And to be honest, I had nowhere else to go.

"That first week was trying. This was before smoking was banned in government buildings, and Donald would come into my office with his beer belly hanging over my desk and a cigarette hanging out of his mouth. He couldn't stand on the opposite side of the room. He had to crowd me by leaning over my shoulder. As he talked, his cigarette ash got longer and longer until it dropped onto a recently completed report or memo. I put out an ashtray, but he couldn't be bothered. I developed a migraine headache and felt really irritated, but it seemed a petty fight to pick, and not the moment for it either.

"Yet after a day or two, I had to admit to some ambivalence regarding him. Donald was no Gregory Peck, but he had an aura of decisiveness and authority about him that was attractive."

"Power can be seductive," said Moira. "You felt excited when he was around?"

"I wouldn't like to admit it," replied Shirley. "All the same, I found myself wanting to please.

"His first request was for a briefing on the impact of a devaluation of the peso on American business operations in Mexico and on prospects for new investment. He asked me to have it ready by Monday morning. So I told friends I was ill, in order to escape a Saturday night engagement, and worked all weekend on the paper. This was something I was good at; I knew what I was doing. I was going to impress the hell out of him. I ended up with a six-page, single-spaced memo with ten pages of relevant tables and analysis attached.

"I went in on Monday morning, exhausted but pleased with my work, some of the best I had done. I had to rely on estimates, but the methodology was clear and I had arrived at my conclusions in a transparent way.

"That day I myself learned how the bureaucratic game is played at the highest levels. I had prepared a concise ten minute briefing, but I never got to first base. In fact, I don't think Donald ever looked at that memo, or any of the others I prepared for him over the next week. Hardly had I entered his office when he started complaining about working all weekend and arriving at the office at five A.M. Oneupmanship! Not a word of encouragement, not even a polite inquiry about my weekend. Donald was totally focused on himself. I felt a mixture of disappointment and resentment. His eyes were bloodshot, and I wondered if this was from substance abuse or whether it really reflected the sleepless nights of a workaholic. I imagined his wife as dull and submissive and I was proved right when she stopped by the office later that week. She was a petite, 1950s-style housewife, and I could see her stroking his ego and picking up his socks every morning.

"Anyway, having elicited my sympathy, Donald then co-opted me into sitting in his office for an hour while he marked his territory like a tomcat. He phoned everyone in the Bureau at the director level and said he had the Secretary's instructions to make a big push on foreign investment. He asked for a meeting with each of them to see how they could help him with this mandate.

"But when, over the next few days, we called on the other directors, they weren't allowed a word in edgewise. Donald had developed a presentation that he delivered verbatim to each director. It had to do with himself, his importance, and the importance of what he was doing. I felt awkward and embarrassed. Why was I dragged along? Had he worked in Japan, where no official worth his salt goes to a meeting unaccompanied by an underling? Or was he in some way showing me off? I knew I was no office center-page spread, but I was known among my peers as, well, pretty smart. Perhaps he recognized that a sharp, clued-in woman could help his career. Or was he perhaps attracted to me? I felt alert and vibrant when I was with him.

"Then Donald left on a two-week business trip.

"That afternoon I got a call from personnel saying that a colleague, Richard Harrington, would be taking over my job, as Donald had wanted someone more 'authoritative.'

"Authoritative! He hadn't even looked at my work! I was told I had two days to find a new job within the Bureau. If not, I could be made redundant and replaced by a political appointee.

"Unlike most bureaucrats, I had always known how lucky we were. The rest of the world saw us as living in an ivory tower, with cushy, protected jobs and good pensions. And it was true. Yes, you pulled in a higher salary in the private sector, but we normally had job security, at least at the lower levels. Once I got my first government appointment, I just moved from one position to another. But now I was more senior, there was less security, and I dreaded the prospect of job hunting: cold calls, unanswered messages, fruitless interviews.

"So I phoned a few colleagues and asked for advice. Fortunately my panic was short-lived. One colleague suggested the Department of International Trade and Commerce. The DITC had a senior advisor vacancy. The announcement had circulated two weeks before and the closing date was that day. I knew Steve, the director. In fact, we had just been to see him. So I called and told him the news.

"'I've just offered the job to someone, but I'd rather have you. I didn't know you were available,' Steve said.

"'Neither did I,' I replied. 'But if you can swing it, I'd love to join your group.' And that's how I ended up in the Department of International Trade and Commerce.

"I had just been hauled from the sea into a lifeboat, but I was hurt and puzzled. It was the first time I had put heart and soul into my job, not just out of professional pride, but to impress someone. And I had been rejected. No explanation, no 'man-to-man' discussion about his requirements or my qualifications. A good manager would have done that, sat me down and had an adult discussion. No, he snuck away like a coward and let a junior personnel officer tell me I was fired. With all my heart I despised him, the foul-breathed, obese, son-of-a-bitch. . . ."

Shirley paused to regain her composure. The hot afternoon sun was beating down on the treeless valley, and everyone silently took a swig of water.

"Eventually Steve left, and he recommended me as his replacement. Being a director has its advantages. For the first time in my life, I refused to give in to Parkinson's law, that work expands to fill the time available. I had gotten where I wanted to be and I was going to have a life. So I arrived a half hour early and left on time. By this time I had been around a good twenty years, so I knew the ropes. Someone once said, it's not what you produce by your work but what you become through it that counts. I became tough and cynical.

"The director's job was a natural for me. I'm good at delegation, overloading the good performers and giving the bad performers busywork to get them out of the way. And I got the details right. For example, I organized the file cabinets into a separate room, locked at night. I wasn't going to be caught for breach of security and I wanted to keep control, know who was looking at what. This proved to be a useful precaution. I arranged for a check-out system and assigned it to Peggy, my most meticulous and loyal staffer. Anyone wanting classified documents had to go through her as her desk was right out-side the file office.

"Over the next year I made sure I followed current bureau-cratic policies. I increased staff diversity by hiring a Chinese-American programmer and an African-American office man-ager. I instituted a management feedback system but made it informal so I could find out what staff thought about me and use it as I thought fit. I established two focus groups to re-view some new strategies I had in mind, and I included rep-resentation from other departments in the groups to look col-legial. One trick I learned was to assign a loyal aide to draft the minutes of meetings ahead of time, reflecting the out-come I wanted. Then I would steer the meeting to conform to the minutes. It's an effective way of promoting your own agenda.

"I soon developed a reputation for success. I was well viewed by the Secretary and, eighteen months after my appointment, when Donald decided to leave the Bureau for a high-paying consultant's job, his department was merged with mine. We became the Department of International Trade, Commerce, and Overseas Investment, or DITCOI for short. I knew I had made it. The firing still rankled, but I felt I had pulled even with Donald.

"The merger of the two departments went smoothly. I was quick and I was 'authoritative.' If there's one advantage to a bureaucracy, it's a clearly defined chain of command and strict accountability. I knew this and I knew how to play the politi-cal game, focusing on results and not getting caught up in showy efforts at reform.

"Professors at business schools enhance their careers by inventing management fads that are seized on as new answers to old problems. Donald was a prime example of a person who would turn a department upside down, introducing current fashions like 'matrix management' or 'hoteling,' and letting someone else sort out the mess. Well, that wasn't my style. It was fine to be decisive, but, to me, 'authoritative' meant using good judgment, not just throwing your weight around.

"Sometimes I had to use bureaucratic tactics to get my way. For example, when senior management wanted to introduce flexible hours, I attended meetings and nodded wisely in agreement at appropriate moments. Then I returned to my office and made sure to present the idea in an unappealing way, to the point where the staff objected fiercely. In the end, I was able to leave things as they were, but I looked good to my boss, who saw me as a team player, and to the staff, who saw me as sensitive to their concerns. That's how office politics worked and I was rather good at it.

"Well, back to Donald. Shortly after he joined the consulting firm, he had the nerve to contact me for some interoffice memos he remembered from his time as director of the DOI. He greeted me on the phone as if we were long-lost friends. For a moment I thought he was about to recall fondly the time we worked together, and I searched for a cutting rejoinder. But the reminiscences never came. He was far too short of time. Meanwhile, I was correct and cooperative.

"Dealing with Congress is a big part of any job of responsibility in government. It's also the most boring task in the civil service. Congressmen are constantly asking for written responses to questions we've answered a thousand times already, and of course they want answers that will satisfy each of their several constituencies. The memos Donald asked for revealed nothing startling, just explanations to Congress on DOI operations. They were unclassified and I could think of no good reason to say no. I sensed he was just trying to establish a precedent for future requests. I gave him what he wanted. At least it got him off my back.

"Six months later he made a more serious request. But this requires some explanation. Donald's clients in his new high-paying consulting job were big companies and development authorities in France. Their mandate was to attract and often negotiate foreign investment from countries not belonging to the European Union, like the US, Japan and Korea. In serving these clients, Donald drew heavily on his knowledge of US companies and their approach to overseas investment, knowledge he had gained while working at the Bureau.

"It so happened that around this time several EU countries were complaining about the disproportionate amount of foreign investment ending up in the UK. Now there are a number of reasons why investors may prefer the UK. English is an international language, British labor laws are less rigid, and London is an attractive city to live in. But these countries claimed that the British were giving unfair incentives, and so a committee was set up to investigate these allegations. There is no EU equivalent of the American Freedom of Information Act, and secrecy is endemic to the workings of Brussels. In this case, the usual blanket of confidentiality descended on the matter.

"The head of the investigative committee was an employee of the German central bank, and the committee's working paper was prepared in his office in Bonn. Now, for some years, our people had had a 'correspondent' (in other words, a spy) in the German central bank, as we routinely had elsewhere. So no sooner had the working paper been produced than I received a copy, which I locked up carefully in the Top Secret file under Peggy's supervision. The contents were dynamite.

"Donald, who had his sources, heard about the committee and also about the working paper. Soon after I received it, he gave me a call and asked to see it. Of course Donald's clients wanted to see the paper in order to lobby for proposals they favored before any decisions were taken. This time I held my ground. I told him I knew of no such paper, but were it to exist, it would be classified and I could not let him see it. Under my breath I said, 'You think you can just fire me and then ask for favors! You've got another think coming.'

"Well, Donald was determined, and the next thing I knew he had contacted the Undersecretary, who called me to his office. By this time I was well established within the bureaucracy as a savvy player. I had my arguments worked out.

"'Yes,' I said, 'the paper does exist, and it's a bombshell. It provides details of what some EU countries consider to be unfair incentives offered by the British to foreign investors. The recommendations are to penalize the British and issue specific EU directives to prevent such incentives in the future.

As we all know, the British may be the most contentious within the EU, but they are also the most compliant with EU regulations. This could be a major blow to their economy.'

"'But let Donald see a copy. After all, he worked here for years.'

"'I would, except that I see this as a matter of national interest. American industry wants as many investment incentives as possible. We certainly don't want to leak the report and help the French destroy the investment incentives US firms enjoy in Britain. That would be shooting our own side in the foot.'

"'I see your point. . . .'

"'I propose we warn the British and share this working paper with them immediately. Let them know we support them, and give them time to marshal a rebuttal.'

"'That makes sense. I'll tell Donald he has to deal with you.'

"And he did have to deal with me. How nice it was to be able to thwart Donald in a major way. Donald, typically, had exuded confidence. I heard through the grapevine that he told his clients, 'I'll have a copy of the report for you within forty-eight hours. Don't worry, I know the right people. That's what you pay me for.' But the forty-eight hours went by and Donald did not have the paper. Three weeks later Donald *still* did not have the paper, despite endless hours on the phone.

"At this point a press conference was held. The British had had time to politic among the EU members in the usual byzantine manner of these things, and the resulting communiqué confined itself to general expressions of future intent, losing the readers in Community gobbledygook. The proposals to curb British incentives were watered down and rendered ineffective in practical terms.

"Now, it may seem like a small thing, but in the world of well-paid consultants the ability to deliver is highly prized. Having promised to obtain the report early on and help the French lobby for stronger sanctions against the British, Donald lost credibility and face. In other words, he blew it! He now had to work harder and harder to satisfy his clients. And then he had a heart attack.

"You could say I should feel sorry for Donald, but I didn't. The s.o.b. was arrogant and hypocritical. Pretending to support me, then knifing me from behind. Requesting extensive analysis and never reading my briefings. Strutting around the Bureau like a feudal lord deigning to show himself to the peasants. No, I felt no pity.

"My greatest pleasure came six months later when Donald applied to re-enter the Bureau as a senior advisor in my department. His doctor had advised him to take a less demanding job. This meant going back to a government job. Overseas investment was what he could do best. As far as I knew, it was *all* he could do. The Undersecretary called me to his office.

"'Shirley,' he said. 'I don't know how comfortable you are with Donald, but he needs a job. I'd like you to take him on as a senior advisor. You know he's been ill, and he doesn't have any other options at the senior advisor level.'

"'Yes, I know,' I said. 'I'd like to help, but my department is coming up for review under the "reinvention of government" program. The Bureau would be heavily criticized if I took on another senior civil service officer, with rights to a pension and full benefits. And if Congress gets wind that we gave a civil service appointment to a former consultant supporting reduced investment incentives for American businessmen in the EU, we could be tied up for months with testimony. I suggest we hire Donald as a consultant. Let's give him the job of a visiting lecturer rather than academic tenure, so to speak. Fewer questions will be raised and we'll still be able to help him out.' I knew my case was impregnable.

"'I knew I could count on you, Shirley. I'll tell Donald to get in touch.'

"When Donald got in touch, I could taste blood. I was cordial but businesslike. I suggested he prepare a proposal for a consultant's report on stimulating American investment overseas. I gave him no hints as to how such a proposal should be structured. After all, he was the consultant, not me.

"Within a week Donald came into the office with his proposal. I told him I was terribly busy and would have to get back to him. The proposal was low on substance and methodology, as I knew it would be. So I wrote Donald a formal letter indicating what additional work needed to be done for his proposal to be considered. Donald resubmitted it after several weeks and our dance was repeated. I was on safe ground. Donald was a good talker and persuasive, but report writing was not his forte.

"Two months later, while the Undersecretary was tied up in some intensive Congressional testimony, I knew the time was ripe. Donald had recently submitted the third draft of his proposal. Meanwhile I had solicited a second proposal on the same subject from a professor I knew at Columbia University Business School. The professor was well qualified and his proposal was excellent. I called the director of personnel to my office.

"'Donald has prepared three drafts of a proposal for a report I need done, but the drafts give me no confidence that he can actually do the work. Call him and tell him we'll have to give the contract to someone else.'

"'He's bound to ask why. What shall I tell him?'

"'Tell him we need someone more "authoritative,"' I said."

Shirley's listeners regarded her with a new-found respect. But the stark landscape around them weighed upon their souls. It was time to move on.

~ The Personal Trainer's Tale ~

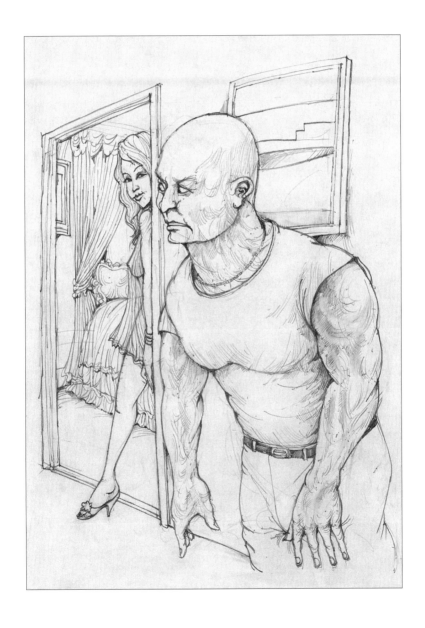

Darryl

Here is a trainer, master of the gym,
Rock-hard biceps, buttocks neat and trim;
Neck like an ox, and shiny, shaven head;
Gait of a primate, a nibbling quadruped.
No model's face, but oozing sex and power,
This Atlas could go on for half an hour.
Or so his female clients fantasize,
Working on their pecs, their abs, and thighs.
A frisson of desire greets his approach,
Alas, his manner is beyond reproach.
Resigned to looking for more wimpish fare
They smile, and nonetheless primp up their hair,
Adjust their limbs to cast to best effect
Those charming parts which show the least defect.
To them he is a listener, gallant;
They wish he were their private confidant.

Sutri, known as the "Gate of Etruria," was one of the early
Roman frontier posts against the Etruscans. We visited the
thirteenth century duomo, walked down the hill, and entered
a large Roman amphitheater, said to have held four thousand
seated and seven thousand standing. One could still distin-
guish the royal box and *vomitoria,* the openings in the stadium
that allowed large numbers of people to enter and leave.

"This wasn't just for theater, surely," said Richard, as the group settled down for a picnic lunch on the old stone steps. "It must have been used for animal fights and gladiators."

"A grisly way to make a living," said Gerald.

"Bear in mind, gladiators were the football stars of ancient Rome," said Jeremy. "Everything about them, their health, their ranking, their state of mind, was followed by an adoring public. And they had their pick of women, rich Roman matrons vying for their attention. Couldn't have been that bad!"

"Lives were brutal, but short. But then lives were short for everyone in those days," said Nigel, reflectively.

"What does our modern gladiator think?" asked Shirley in an unexpected overture to Darryl.

"You mean, would I have liked being a gladiator? I'd have survived. The winners were the ones who used their brains," said Darryl, taking a double helping of lean turkey and salad on nine-grain bread.

Lizzie flashed a smile. "Like some mayo on that?"

"No thank you. This is low-cal. But it still has some bulk. I have to balance out the fats with enough protein and carbo."

"Go on, you're on vacation," said Shirley.

"We're almost in Rome, Darryl, and we haven't heard what it's like to be a personal trainer," said Lizzie.

"And what it's like to be admired by hundreds of body-conscious women." This was Nicola.

"You and Gerald are the only ones who haven't told a story," added Richard.

"All right," said Darryl, laughing. "I get the point! I'll tell you everything.

"I'm an early riser, always have been. Wake up at five-thirty, down to the gym by six. A quick cup of coffee before leaving the house, then a good breakfast 'round eight. It's my power meal: three eggs, boiled or scrambled, whole wheat toast, a bowl of raisin bran, two or three bananas and a couple of apples. Then I'm grazing most of the day, like I tell the clients; small, but often. It's tempting to do the quick and easy thing, you know, burgers, fries, and chips. But diet's king in my line of work. I usually try to have a small stock of nuts, dried fruit, that sort of thing. Energy bars, too.

"I put in about forty minutes of cardio and several sets of abs in the morning. Then 'round lunchtime I do the serious work, about thirty minutes of progressive push-pull weight resistance. The more muscle you put on, the more your metabolism speeds up and the more you need to eat."

"Quite a routine! You must get bored," said Jeremy.

"Bored? No, not bored, but it *can* become addictive. There's a lot of people in the business like that. As for myself, I work out five, maybe six, days a week, but take a break on the weekends. You know, a movie, some errands. It's dumb, getting burned out and never wanting to see the inside of a gym again."

"How did you get into personal training?" asked Randall.

"I grew up in Pittsburgh. My mother was a strict Catholic. My father was a steelworker. He was big. Fat, actually. My whole family was fat. Dad used to come home tired at night and just bum down on the couch in front of the tube. He could stay there for the rest of the day, the weekend too, a football fan who never walked farther than the fridge. I swore I'd never be like that. From the time I was a kid, I played every sport I came across and ended up captain of the football team. Dad was proud of me. He even came out to watch me play. Of course, he also spent time checking out the coeds.

"I guess I had my pick. One time we went on a league tour of Pennsylvania high schools and had to stay in motels. The cheerleaders came with us and stayed in a separate motel down the road, with a couple of chaperones. They, like, snuck out at night and we'd drink and watch videos. It was no big deal, except that one night some of them came scratching on my window after I'd turned in. When I opened the door they pulled me over to the bed, waving a bottle of Southern Comfort. There were three of them, high on booze or whatever and wearing raincoats with some skimpy underwear underneath. I started to protest but one said 'It's okay, we're on the pill.' The prettiest one had her hand where she shouldn't. 'Who do you want first?' she asked. 'I bet Sheri and Norma it'd be me.'"

Darryl had our attention. Those of us farther away on the steps inched in closer. He continued.

"Now, don't get me wrong, they were cute, but only about fifteen or sixteen, and all of them chewing gum. I can't kiss a gum chewer. I lay there, limp as a wet loofah and asked if their parents knew where they were. That ended my reputation as a stud.

"But don't worry. That night aside, I got plenty of action. I must have learned more about sex by the time I was eighteen than most men do by the time they're thirty. And I enjoyed it like hell, especially with the older girls who had a little technique along with the enthusiasm. Unlike the young ones, they wouldn't necessarily think they were in love, which is another thing. I wasn't ready for that. I was in love, but with feeling fit, being professional, earning some money, and having my own space.

"Pittsburgh wasn't a good place to be at that time, with the steel industry declining and the place looking sort of run down. I joined the Marines for peace and quiet (I'm not joking) and they paid for my college degree, the first in my family. I majored in exercise physiology and later did clinical nutrition in Cincinnati. When I left the service, I threw myself into strength training and took the American Council on Exercise certification, something we all have to have. Then I took the National Strength Professionals Association certification and went on to specialize in accident avoidance, raising bone density, and strengthening ligaments and tendons, that sort of thing. People think we're just muscle men, but we have to keep up with what's going on in the field.

"I had to start somewhere, so I moved to Texas and did house calls for several years. There's good money in it, and it's easy to get into. After four or five years you can get liability insurance for almost nothing, like a hundred and sixty dollars a year. I started off with male clients. Men prefer a male trainer, the bigger the better. But some men're a real pain in the neck, you know, the kind of guy who just wants you to tell him how great he is or the kind of guy who thinks you're a wimp if you're shorter than he is. 'Hey, Arnold Schwarzenegger, shake in your boots,' one said to me. And then there was the guy who wanted me to get him some hormone precursors, DHEA, and rostenedione, the stuff they use in the Olympics. 'Banned, unnecessary, and potentially harmful,' I told him. He told me to get lost.

"I ended up having more female clients than male. Women are generally happy with a trainer of either sex. Of course, some are just trying to keep up with the Joneses. You know, the sort of woman who says, 'Amy told me you gave her an hour's workout using five pound weights and no cardio. That's what I want.' Well, that's fine if you go jogging three times a week like Amy, but it doesn't make sense if you don't. Then there's the type that uses you as a weapon in some undeclared marital war, the type who tells her husband, 'Darryl thinks he and I should be getting together more often' and then watches his expression.

"Usually, though, women are into improvement. They listen and get results. Of course, you hear a lot about their personal problems in the course of the workout. I find the abs part at the end usually elicits a complaint about something—finances, relationships, office politics. After a while some clients begin to treat you like a friend, which you're not. You've got to be sympathetic but play it straight. Look too interested or touch them in the wrong place and you can get into trouble. Especially since the best advertisement is word of mouth and often a lot of your clients will know each other. Only one woman has to complain and her friends will suddenly remember some harmless little joke or aside, an accidental brushing of the breasts. Suited me. I played it straight, but sometimes it wasn't so easy. I'll give you an example.

"I was several months into my private consulting when I visited an older female client, in her early forties. I had moved to the gulf coast, the eastern part near Galveston, and on that particular day there was a hurricane warning. The clouds were threatening and most people were closing up, staying inside. In retrospect I should have stayed home, but I had an appointment and the woman said she wanted to keep it. So I turned up at her house and took her through the usual routine.

"Toward the end of the session I realized the skies were darkening and the wind, gale force when I had arrived, was strengthening. 'Stay for lunch,' my client suggested, 'it makes no sense driving in these conditions.' We ate smoked salmon and salad and had a glass of wine. I got up from the table a starving man, but I just joked about drinking in the middle of the day, and we laughed.

"All of a sudden there was an almighty roar and a ripping sound. A huge gust of wind tore open the screen door to the kitchen. We looked out the glass panel in the door and saw that the garage roof had been torn off and hurled about someplace. Debris was flying about, so I manhandled a sofa into the kitchen to reinforce the door and told my client to hide under the dining room table.

"At this point she started getting hysterical. If the storm could demolish the garage, it could wreck the house. She was right, but there wasn't much we could do about it. Fortunately, hysteria in others makes me feel calm and in command. She was terrified and shivering, so I found a blanket and wrapped her in it. I crouched down beside her under the dining room table, listening to the howling wind and the crashing objects hitting houses, trees and vehicles at random.

"The hurricane abated and the rain lashed down. My client grew calm, but I realized she was snuggling closer and closer for comfort. I made to get up but she clung to me. I had my suspicions, but on the other hand it had been a pretty terrifying moment. I got up to look outside. The wind had moderated. Maybe it was still dangerous, but I was anxious to get going.

"'Please don't go yet,' she said.

"So I stayed. And as I lay still beneath the table, she removed some of the blanket and threw it over me. I realized then that in the time it had taken me to look outside, she had undressed. Her exercise kit lay in a tangle at her feet. Beneath the blanket she was quite naked, and there were goosebumps on her arms and breasts. She moved onto her side and laid her arm across my chest.

"'Darryl, hold me,' she said. 'I'm frightened.'

"She nuzzled up to me. I felt real protective, like a stag with a doe. Sex with clients can happen in any personal service profession, and the exercise industry is no exception. But I knew the risk. Sometimes honesty is the best course.

"'I'm lucky to find you as a client,' I said. 'I look forward to our sessions. But I can't afford to get intimate. I just can't mix that with the job. Let's blame the weather, shall we? Hey, come here.'

"And I held her real tight and stayed with her a while until the feelings subsided and gave space for a new mood to catch on. I wish I was better at these things. But she was a nice woman and kind at heart. I got away with it and kept her business. But as soon as I left her house that day, I went to a barbecue and had myself a large serving of ribs and rice and gravy."

The sun was heating up, and Nigel and Shirley took out their hats and sunscreen. Others followed suit. No one wanted to move just yet.

"I wasn't so lucky the second time around. I had an arrangement to visit a young woman called Rosa on a Tuesday evening. Usually I would arrive at the house, ring the bell, and she'd let me in. She'd complain about her job selling medical supplies, driving up to three hundred miles a day, and then we'd get down to business. On the day in question I arrived at the house and saw a post-it note stuck to the front door.

"'Darryl, the door's open. Come on in.'

"I went in. There was nobody around. I sat down and waited. Then I heard a woman singing. I moved quietly to the bottom of the stairs and heard a song with salsa rhythm, faint but clear over the sound of a shower.

"'Damn,' I thought, 'she's gonna make me late.'

"I sat down again and idly glanced through some magazines on a table. Right there, in full view, were a bunch of porno magazines with young muscle-bound men in obscene poses. I'd been around—in the Marines, dammit—but I'd never seen stuff like that before. I waited another ten minutes, then heard a voice from the top of the stairs:

"'Darryl, are you down there?'

"'Good guess! Since seven thirty, on the dot.' I sounded grumpy and felt it.

"'You should've told me you were here!'

"'You were in the shower.'

"'So?' answered the disembodied voice.

"'I don't wander upstairs while the client's taking a shower.'

"'Oh, don't be so stuffy, Darryl. We're friends,' said Rosa, appearing in a sheer dress that looked almost like a nightgown. I could see through to her breasts, and they seemed larger and heavier than I would have imagined. I became aware of my own body and knew I was in trouble. I was used to cute butts and sexy legs, but covered in lycra.

"'Put on your gear. I'll be late for my next appointment as it is.'

"'Poor Darryl, so conscientious. Can't you have just poco-poco bit of fun for a change?'

"Half a bottle of expensive perfume wafted through the house as she spoke with a strong, husky accent.

"'In Colombia, a healthy man never turns down a young woman.'

"Rosa sat herself down on the sofa across from me, letting her diaphanous dress ride up her legs. In the light, I thought I could see a dark patch through her dress, but I tried not to think about it.

"'In fact,' she continued, 'if he heard me in the shower, he'd take off his clothes and join me. He'd soap my back and enjoy the slippery feel of my body touching his. Maybe then he'd. . . .'

"'He'd what?' I asked, preparing for exit but curious about Colombian customs. A tempting voice whispered in my head, 'Go on, Darryl. Look at those nipples! Who'll find out?'

"'He'd take a soft towel,' she continued, 'and dry me off slowly, stroking my shoulder with one hand and rubbing gently between my legs with the other. Do you know what this does to a woman, Darryl? Then he'd carry me to the bed, Darryl, his hardness gently brushing my lower back. I would sigh as he spread me among the sheets and pillows, my nipples taut, every inch of me yearning. His lips would be moist and his heart would be pumping. . . .'

"'Maybe, but *after* working hours,' I interrupted as I snapped back into self-control mode. *This woman's been reading too much pulp fiction. Where did she get this crap?* She was too much.

"'Yanqui puritan!' she yelled, as I fled the house. I jumped into the car and pulled out a bag of Cheerios. I had a career to think about."

"Darryl, how many encounters like that did you have?" asked Moira.

"Oh, there's others," said Darryl, reaching for some cheese and grapes. "But I'll tell you about the worst one.

"A client introduced me to a young woman who wanted to switch trainers. She said her boyfriend thought she'd work harder with a 'good looking' personal trainer. I have a reputation as a crack trainer and I thought she was just trying to flatter me with the 'good looking' part. I didn't want to be uncooperative, and you do hear some weird reasons for people wanting to work out. Why should I care?

"I got her jogging in the park, doing crunches and lifting weights. Three sessions went by and all was well. Then on the fourth session she opened the door with a housecoat on. I thought nothing of it, until I came in and saw a guy there. She unzipped the housecoat and I could see she was stark naked.

"'I don't do threesomes,' I said on the way out. 'And I'm not that good looking!' I jumped in the car and went straight for some nuggets and slaw.

"After that, I gave up house calls. No kidding, I suppose you'd call me a straight arrow. Private business was a hassle at the best of times—driving everywhere, getting the clients to pay, and keeping appointments at the crack of dawn, or evenings and weekends. But handling this type of 'come on.' Well, I decided to join a gym.

"Gyms are great. If you can build your clientele and get up to twenty or thirty hours of personal training in a two-week period, the gym will give you a regular salary with benefits. And you can increase your income if you get into management, as I did. Mind you, you have to watch the trainer-client relationships. All gyms get the occasional Lothario. You can watch the body language and just know trouble's brewing. We kick those guys out. Really. Clients notice. They might look like they're concentrating on their repetitions, but they see what's going on around them and get embarrassed seeing people turning on to each other."

"Sounds like you've got it made in Texas," said Randall, adjusting his sunglasses and flashing a smile. "What brought you on a trip like this?"

"I needed a break. It's all been, for me, a rather upsetting experience. I wasn't going to talk about it, but I don't have any other story to tell. The trouble is, we're all human. You're brought up with certain values and you try to live by them, do the right thing. I know I tend to see things in black and white, and can be real judgmental at times. This is right, that's wrong, and so on. Maybe I get some comfort from feeling certain. And maybe I feel superior when I resist temptation. It's something I guess I get from my mother's side. I don't really believe in that much casual sex when you're an adult, and definitely don't approve of sex with married women. As I say, I'm a straight, law-abiding type, even though I sowed a few oats while I was growing up. But if God had wanted us to be hermits alone in a cave, he wouldn't have given us irresistible women. I'm referring to Anita. I'm now more sympathetic with trainers who get drawn into a relationship they weren't looking for. I'm less sure about things since I met her.

"Anita came to the gym a year and a half ago. She was about forty, with the figure of a sixteen-year-old. She was as flexible as a ballet dancer, but said she wanted more strength and stamina. I had a full schedule, but Anita said she'd wait until I had a free slot. So I became her personal trainer.

"I realized from the start that Anita was not just another client for me. I was less assertive and matter-of-fact with her, and I was more interested in what she had to say. Physically she was different from other women coming to the gym. She had long dark hair and wore it in a variety of ways, from a Farrah Fawcett look to braids crossed on top. Her dress style was sleek and rich, what I'd call the European look, with perfect nails and knit tops. But it wasn't just her appearance. She was more confident, more sophisticated. She had traveled after college, to places like southern India and Hong Kong. And she had majored in English and taught a course called 'Survey of English Literature' at a local community college before getting married.

"Anita was the sort of self-assured woman who feels at home in any culture and any situation. One minute she'd be telling me about the art exhibits in London museums and the next minute she'd be laughing at some silly joke she found on the internet. I love a sense of humor; you don't get much of it in my business. Clients are generally serious and results-driven, when they're not holding forth about their latest gripes. Anita laughed a lot and when she smiled she'd close her eyes, like, for just a moment. Then she'd slowly open them and gaze at you sideways from under her eyelids. It was very flirtatious.

"I designed a well-balanced workout for her, with cardio, weights, and stretching. Women need weights when they get to a certain age, you know, it helps maintain bone density. Anyway, during her second or third workout, she started to complain about a pain in her shoulder. I had seen this before; it's caused by muscles getting torn or irritated. You have to know about that sort of thing in my profession. She was impressed, I could tell.

"'What can I do?'

"'The trick is to strengthen the muscles around the rotator cuff,' I replied. 'Massage helps, too. It keeps the muscles supple while they're being strengthened.'

"'Would you just put your hand there and massage it a little?' she asked, removing the shoulder strap of her tank top. I hesitated.

"For years I had resisted involvement with clients and I realized now the reason why. I had always been in control, had never felt overpowered by a situation. The work had come first and I had trained myself to suppress random thoughts and emotions, to concentrate on the technical aspects of the work regardless of age, sex, or anything else. This was different, somehow more intimate, as if there were a forcefield around us, making us invisible to others. There was no special secret between us, but I knew instinctively that soon there might or would be, and I felt disinclined to fight the feeling.

"It was the first time I touched her. I remember thinking how brown her skin was, a slight freckling and no strap marks.

"'I'm going to touch it now, is that all right?' I asked. You can never be too careful.

"'Mmmh, that's good,' she said, turning her head and giving me one of those lidded smiles.

"I could see Anita found me attractive. When she asked me to make a house call, I decided to make an exception. I told myself I needed to get out of the gym, have a break from the endless pop music and sweaty bodies. But it was more than just a break in routine, more than curiosity. It was compulsion.

"Anita's husband was a successful banker, some twenty years older than her, and they lived in a large house in an exclusive suburb. No children. I parked the car on the road, walked up the gravel driveway, and stepped into another world. There was never any pretense about working out. I think we both knew what was going to happen and neither of us agonized about it.

"She led me up to a bedroom with a large bay window and plush wall-to-wall carpeting. I didn't refuse the suggestion to go upstairs. In fact, I didn't refuse any of her suggestions. I abandoned my personal values, my self-discipline, and my professional code. I surrendered to my basic instincts, and there was no thunderbolt from heaven. There was no awkwardness, no athleticism, no frustration. Despite her sophisticated manner, Anita was as soft and gentle as an angel. And I just waited for her and that was fine. I'm not sure anyone had done that before.

"Blissful days followed. Weekends were out since her husband worked at home then. But I managed to escape the gym three or four afternoons a week during my Monday-to-Friday schedule and I'd drive out to Anita's house. It wasn't easy, and I'd sometimes lie about where I was going. But I got away with it.

"Each encounter was a 'first time' experience. Not because Anita had to worry about keeping me interested. In fact, I rather like the comfort of a familiar situation and if the sex works, and it usually does for me, I've never fussed about the surroundings. I guess it was something she did to amuse herself. It was just part of who she was. The change of scene was sometimes dramatic—a velvet robe, colored lights, and incense—and sometimes it was subtle, like daisies in a vase.

"Anita loved music and used it for atmosphere. The music was like a discreet voyeur, joining us in our intimacy while remaining in the background. One day it would be Russian folksongs, sung by a deep and dirty bass, more elemental than Robert Johnson's blues. Another time it was English madrigals, sung solo or by groups and evoking the misty quaintness of those bygone times Anita admired. In fact, her selections spanned the ages, from the forty or so fragments of music from ancient Greece to the minimalism of Philip Glass, who, by the way, is someone I could relate to. And let me tell you, this Glass stuff is the way to go if you want a sophisticated seduction.

"Whatever the circumstance, I was always ready for her. So critical of others' addictions, I now found myself unable to resist the chance to enter her world, gather up that soft firm flesh and lose myself until the whispered time of our next meeting brought me back into the real world. I was a small fish at the end of Anita's line and she toyed with me, letting out the line, then gently pulling me back. I offered no resistance, either to the coming or the going. I adjusted to her needs and constraints and somehow managed to earn my living at the gym in between visits.

"The sex was great. Sometimes we just settled for missionary position and sometimes we just relaxed in bed. But sometimes Anita would be bursting with energy and she loved the fact that I could pick her up bride-and-groom style and twirl her 'round. Or I might carry her on my hip like a child or hoist her on my shoulders and fondle her breasts. The bedroom was large enough for us to play. The bed itself was in an alcove, but we made full use of the carpeted area in front of the bay window. She loved to pose in a provocative position and make me wait as long as I could and then take her as I found her. All this with the sun streaming in. I assumed the neighbors were not home or, if they were, that we would remain unobserved behind the reflections of the sun and sky upon the windowpanes. But I didn't know for sure.

"From time to time, Anita's husband would spend weekends away on business trips, and I would move in to fill the void in her life. It was an abrupt cultural change for both of us. We—me and Anita—came from different worlds. I talked about management problems and groused about trainers.

Anita talked about English poetry. I didn't know much about poetry, so I asked Anita to suggest some things to read. She gave me some love poems and some poems about nature. Her favorites were by English poets like Marvell, Milton, and Donne. Occasionally, I was struck by what one of them said. Like Milton who asked, 'What is strength without a double share of wisdom?' And a poet called Dryden who said, 'Beware the fury of a patient man.' Interesting. But beyond that it wasn't my thing.

"We continued to spend time together, and then Anita started talking about leaving her husband.

"'Anita,' I said, 'We have different interests, different talents, and different friends.'

"'I think we have more in common than you think,' she replied. 'What you do, you do well. But you're also observant, you're articulate, and you're interested in the world beyond the gym. There's so much more in there,' she murmured, gently stroking my naked chest. 'Believe me, I know what I'm saying.'

"I felt my whole body tense. I could see where she was headed and I didn't like it one bit.

"'Sure,' I said. 'I know there's a world beyond the gym, and I like reading, but it's something I do on the side. I look at some of your books because I want to know what turns you on. But this poetry stuff's not my thing. I don't even understand some of it!'

"'It doesn't have to be poetry.'

"*But something more intellectual than working out,* I thought.

"You have to understand. I was brought up in a working environment. Men were men and they did things with their hands. What couldn't be done by honest toil wasn't worth doing. The fancy people in New York or Boston—lawyers, managers and so on—were regarded as, well, snobs, maybe even pansies. 'Brainwork's no work' was the motto. Take music for example. Anita would listen to her tapes, react in ecstasy to every climax and smile at every resolution. But she couldn't play an instrument. Me, well, I like rock and some country. But if I can't actually play it or sing it, I'm not going to spend a lot of time with it.

"English literature, where does that get you? I earn more demonstrating the leg press than Anita could ever earn lecturing on English poets, assuming she needed to. History? The only date I've ever been interested in is one on two legs. No, action's the thing, making a difference, having a role in something concrete.

"'Journalism, then,' Anita suggested one afternoon as we sat lounging in some easy chairs drinking homemade smoothies.

"'Yeah, well, okay,' I said. 'Journalism's doing, not theorizing, I give you that. And writing, now that's something concrete. I like words and my vocabulary is all right. I even know some Italian.'

"I had fantasies of a new life. I pictured myself rushing to cover a bomb scare for the local newspaper, watching a police chase from a helicopter, or investigating a drug ring. I had visions of standing before a microphone accepting a Pulitzer

Prize, generously ascribing my success to a handpicked team of investigators. I also imagined myself covering a US Open (any Open), interviewing top tennis and golf stars or football coaches. Maybe I'd progress to television and become a sports pundit, telling the audience what I would have done if I'd been on the field.

"But then reality intruded. I was thirty-three years old. It's not old, but journalists start young and have relevant degrees. Even sports reporters have some appropriate background, like professional sports.

"Anita said, 'Try it, Darryl. For me.'

"Daydream yielded to nightmare. Three years in journalism school, a latecomer with no experience, I saw in my mind's eye a hundred unanswered job applications, carefully composed and totally useless. I saw months of hanging around at home, networking on the phone, offering free lunches to people I had never met before and would never meet again. And then, I'd be dependent on Anita for income. I had never felt so protective, so in tune, so willing to give. I doubt I'll ever feel about anyone the way I felt about Anita. But I felt threatened by her and her ambitions for me.

"And then my other, unspoken fear was realized. Anita's husband returned home early from a trip to New Mexico. As we lay in bed, half covered by the sheets, I heard the sound of the car drawing into the graveled driveway at the front of the house. There was no time for farewells, much less a shower. I grabbed my track suit and shoes and was fully clothed before Anita had recovered her dressing gown from the jumble of sheets and spreads. Sound of a key in the front door lock. I threw my empty water bottle and a half-eaten energy bar into the trash basket and opened a window onto the back garden. I stood on the window ledge, reached out, and swung over to the downspout, dropping the last four feet to the ground.

"As I sprinted for the safety of my car out in the road, I was overcome with panic and a frantic desire to put that place and time behind me, to be as far away as possible. Guilt was mixed with relief that I hadn't been caught. Shame at my own recklessness and self-indulgence followed shortly afterwards. Breaking up marriages, however routine and loveless they might seem, was not my style.

"Once back home, I lay on my bed and thought more calmly about my time with Anita. The magic had disappeared with the sound of the wheels in the driveway, and there was no question of seeing her again. Sometimes outside events force an issue. But Anita had introduced me to new things and different ways of thinking. I wished I had talked to her more, told her how I felt. But even if her husband had not returned home unexpectedly that afternoon, even if I had not had that embarrassing jump from the bedroom window, and even if I had not felt that onrush of guilt and shame, I would still have known that life with Anita was not to be.

"I guess the ending was inevitable. After all, Donne said, 'Be thine own palace, or the world's thy jail.'"

Darryl paused. "Hey, I think I'll take one of those cream tarts."

‒ The Retired Colonel's Tale ‒

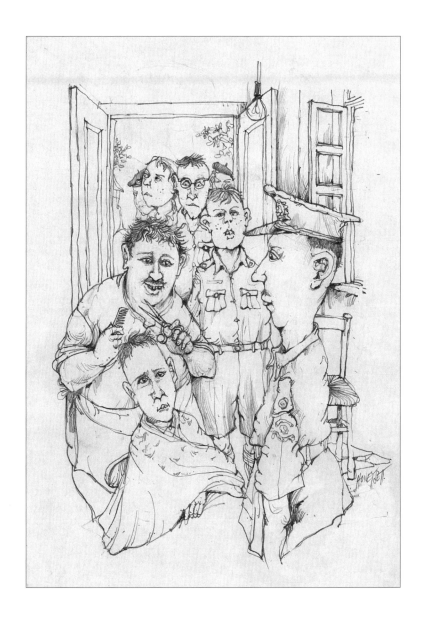

Gerald

The colonel, fresh from modest Cotswold farm,
Is dapper, despite a single useful arm.
His Barbour jacket, customary cladding,
Covers a sweater, sewn with elbow padding.
Although his desk-bound job he rarely misses,
About his early days he reminisces.
When young he was a soldier who'd conform
To discipline and military norm:
"Play by the book, we're paid to win,
Regardless of the futile war we're in.
Obey, don't think, debating wrong from right,
Those who imagine tend to lose the fight."
This is a pro. His mantra, known by rote,
Has slowly morphed into a milder note,
A gentle intimation of regret
About events he'd rather now forget.

Near the end of our walk, we came upon a church shelled
during the war. It was standing alone, on a promontory. The
local people had made their own little chapel nearby in the
open air with votive candles, a Madonna and a rosary arranged
in a niche in an old wall. The altar had been recovered from
the old church, and someone had placed on it a white cloth
and a simple glass vase with fresh flowers. A lectern was made
out of a stump of wood and a brocade cloth, and two crude

benches were arranged for the congregation. We sat there for a moment of silence, our thoughts turning to man's spirit of survival.

We continued on to La Storta, a former military camp on the outskirts of Rome. Gerald went with Moira and Nicola for coffee in the piazza, where they met an old Sicilian parachutist who had fought in Libya during the war. He engaged them in conversation in broken English and surreptitiously handed Nicola and Moira a picture of himself as a young man, with naked torso and a romantic expression. Nicola smiled but turned her back on the old man.

"You must have seen the world, too, Gerald. Tell us about it," said Nicola.

"I've been about a bit. Germany, Hong Kong, Bahrain, hot spots like that." He laughed. "Had a spell in Washington at the embassy there in the seventies. A lot of my career has been fighting the old in-tray and passing the buck to the next fellow. Can't have a fellow like me in the *armed* forces, can we?"

"How did you come to lose your arm?" asked Moira.

"Aden. I was leaning up against my vehicle, map in hand, pointing to a rebel position in the desert hills. The lower arm was a mess, but the amputation was clean. My main problem was learning to use my left hand for everything two hands had coped with before."

"How dreadful." Nicola winced.

"Can't complain, I had an interesting career. In fact, I have a story you may be interested to hear. It dates from my first proper posting, in Cyprus. My assignment was internal security. That's a euphemism for being a glorified policeman. I was twenty-five and a freshly minted second lieutenant."

Jeremy and Richard showed up in the piazza and Nicola waved them over.

"Gerald's telling us a story about his tour of duty in Cyprus forty years ago."

Jeremy and Richard joined them, ordered coffee, and sat back to listen.

"The Congress of Vienna had given Cyprus to Britain some eighty years before, but it was never regarded as more than a 'stationary aircraft carrier,' guarding the approaches to Egypt and India. As usual, we divided and ruled over the Greeks and Turks, who were sleepily content until the army came, at least, if you believe Lawrence Durrell's *Bitter Lemons*. The roads were quite good, I'll grant that, but our maps of the island were hopeless. And we never did much for the locals. By the 1950s the Greek Cypriots were in simmering revolt, demanding *enosis*, or union with Greece, and we had to keep the peace between the communities our predecessors had divided.

"We were shipped out on the *Dunera,* an old bucket that must have transported troops to the Crimea a hundred years before and made them sick back then, too. It would bury its bow in a wave, corkscrew up out of it and judder as if the whole ship were shaking to pieces.

"A few of the men had been in Tonfanau in North Wales doing anti-aircraft gunnery training, yet they were supposed to become an 'internal security force' overnight. One of them told me that while he was there, firing thousands of rounds at drogues, three pilotless towing planes were shot down. The towing planes were three miles in front of their drogues. Need I say more? By the time we arrived in Famagusta, all they knew was how to stop a stranger: 'Halt! *Stamata! Dur!*' I swear, if you didn't watch out some idiot would pick up his loaded .303 rifle the wrong way round and pull the trigger.

"Our camp was in a wood surrounded by Greek and Turkish villages. You could tell them apart because the Greek village would have an orthodox church and the Turkish village would have a mosque with a minaret.

"Cyprus sounds like a romantic place. It's the home of Aphrodite, and Anthony gave the island as a gift to Cleopatra. St. Paul was there, and it was invaded by Alexander, Haroun al Rashid, and Richard Lionheart. But there was little romantic about our situation. The camp was set up with tents and duckboards and little else. Somebody back home in Parliament complained, 'How can we send our brave boys overseas on active service without proper housing, etc.?' So thirty thousand mirrors and thirty thousand little glass ashtrays arrived to improve our living conditions. Bless the Queen! It was chaos. Conscript armies tend to be.

"We had three troops, each numbering forty-two men, and I was a troop commander. Three days after our arrival, twelve soldiers, sent to relieve a police station, were killed by a bomb as they drew up outside the building. The men stopped complaining about the tents and duckboards after that.

"To be honest, the first order of the day for us was not the lay of the land between the Greeks and the Turks but rather an inventory of the young women in the neighborhood. When you get older and more responsible, issues of quarter-mastering, logistics, and guerilla warfare may take precedence. But at that age our consuming interest was, yes, girls. Unfortunately, there wasn't much to choose from. The average age among the locals approached seventy, taking schoolchildren into account!

"Then someone spotted Ariadne. Ariadne was Greek and lived in the nearby village of Yialousa. She was seventeen, with a figure to dream about. She had long, silky black hair and dark brown eyes that she cast downward at the road as she passed you. She wore simple cotton dresses. When I first saw her she was wearing a dress printed with blue and red roses. She appeared to be amused at everything despite her demure behavior. One hundred and twenty young men fell madly in love.

"But the few scowling, suspicious young Greek men in the village were clearly displeased. Not long after we arrived, our commanding officer received a message from the village elders, and I was sent with the battery captain to confront the Greek orthodox priests and the eternal gossips in the village square.

"'*Kopiaste,* we bid you welcome,' they said. 'Sit down with us and enjoy our hospitality.'

"We drank the thick, dark coffee. Then they closed ranks around their most attractive asset.

"'If you want to avoid unnecessary bombings, keep your men away from our young women, and especially young Ariadne.'

"And so the village was placed off limits for rest and recreation. Fraternizing with locals on either side was to be a disciplinary matter. Anyone caught chatting up a young woman would be confined to barracks, his case referred to Regimental HQ. Frankly, I believe in keeping the sexes apart in the military. Don't hold with women on the front line or in the barracks. But for a group of hormone-intensive roosters, strict rules like that made them even more preoccupied with women.

"However, for some things we had to venture into the village. Thursday was haircut day. If we were in camp, soldiers with more than a millimeter of hair would board a one-tonner, and, led by me, would visit the barber in Yialousa. Under peaceful conditions, the village was only seven minutes away but under the current state of alert it required stopping at every culvert or turn in the road, inspecting every rock and gully for bombs or suspicious bottles. Greeks recognized that the British fought beside them in World War II and saw the British as friends. But with the new reality of British weakness and decolonization, Greek Cypriots became dead set on union with Greece. The British government said no. According to Durrell, to disarm a Greek you have only to embrace him. But for me and my troop, there were to be no embraces.

"By the time we had arrived in Cyprus, there was barely a smiling point in common. *Enosis and only enosis* was scrawled, painted, or sprayed on every available wall. Bombs, bullets, stones, and jeers were the common currency, and we could be attacked on any bend in the road. We didn't hang around. Once in Yialousa, we used to do our business as quickly as possible, with an occasional nod to the mustachioed, baggytrousered old men who stared unblinkingly at us from the café.

"Well, the barber had a son called Spirou, who had studied English in school. Like me, he was about nineteen and learning his trade. Out of sight of his peers, and in the privacy of his own home, which served as the barber shop, he would sometimes relax and talk to us, eager to practice his English, content with the easy work over the pudding basin, and glad of the money. The British paid well over the norm for this personal service.

"It was clear that Spirou was smitten with Ariadne. Join the gang, we thought, and envied his easy access to the village beauty. He told us that Ariadne lived with her widowed mother and aunt on the edge of the village in a simple two-room house with ancient sun-bleached wooden doors and a vine covering the porch. An orange grove, with a mixture of ordinary and marmalade oranges, provided the family a means of support. There was a younger brother who led his high school class in demonstrations against the British, and an older brother called Aristotle, or Ari for short, whose occupation was left rather vague.

"I must, by the way, tell you a funny little story about the family. One day I was patrolling near their home. It was hot and we were thirsty. I approached the old mother, dressed in black, her headshawl covering her hair. 'May we buy some oranges?' I asked. Denial and incomprehension. I pointed and held out some money. 'Please,' I said. No, she indicated. At that moment Spirou appeared. 'What do you want?' he asked. 'We are asking to buy some oranges,' I replied. 'Let her give you the oranges. You are visitors, her guests. If you pay you will offend her.' We took the oranges with broad smiles of thanks. The old mother gave a toothy grin. Peeled, they turned out to be marmalade oranges, very bitter to eat!

"Over the months I got to know Spirou a bit, but the hostility to the British within the Greek community remained a barrier between us. Real friendship was impossible, and we had to be careful not to acknowledge each other too overtly. As it was, our periodic visits to his home, albeit for commercial purposes, must have raised suspicions among some of his fellow villagers, or so we thought.

"Imagine then my surprise, not to mention discomfit, when we received intelligence through police sources that Spirou was active in EOKA. EOKA was the Greek Cypriot nationalist organization that sought the end to British rule and was led by the flamboyant Colonel Grivas. We had labeled Grivas a 'terrorist,' of course, and he called us 'the occupiers.' Maybe Spirou was a member out of conviction, or maybe he felt obliged to prove his loyalty to the cause in view of the economic benefits his family enjoyed from the British.

"One day we received a tip-off that there was to be an EOKA meeting near Ayios Simeon, a small village further down the peninsula. We weren't told where the meeting would take place, but doubted it would be in the village itself, under the noses of such informers as we had. I had been on patrol with P Troop two weeks earlier and we had searched some caves among the cliffs above the village. We had found nothing of importance, but fresh footprints in the dusty caves had suggested something more than a couple of shepherds sheltering for the night. Access to the caves from the northern side was treacherous and almost impossible in the dark, and to the south there was a fine view across the valley, from the lemon groves and the carob trees to the endless unspoiled sandy beaches of the Karpass. If I were organising a secret meeting, I thought, this would be an excellent spot. Inaccessible on one side and open countryside on the other, it would give me a good field of fire in the daylight, and maybe in the dark, too.

"I decided to take a gamble and at sunset arrived with eight men outside Ayios Simeon. Sergeant Miller was with me. Miller was a true veteran, attached to us from the Special Air Service. He had been in Malaya during the Communist insurrection and was a trained guerilla fighter, the only man I ever met who really could rub two sticks together and make fire. But on this occasion his real skill was camouflage, the art of blending into the countryside and moving without being spotted. Miller was a natural. He was a huge, burly weight lifter, yet he could vanish from sight without a sound and cross fifty yards of dry, crackly brush without a whisper.

"We moved, the eight of us, to the foot of the cliffs, edging along in the direction of the caves. Then suddenly I knew that my hunch was correct. Several dogs were tied to the stunted olive trees that studded the poor soil. We could see them ahead of us, leashed at fifty-foot intervals. This was a common practice around Greek and Turkish villages. Like the geese of ancient Rome, they were posted to warn of intruders, four-legged and very noisy challengers to every squad of British soldiers bent on searching villages by stealth.

"But this was too far from the village. The dogs could only be there for an unusual reason. The trick was to sneak past them by inching slowly and painfully forward, taking cover behind the mulberry and carob trees, across stones and through the brush, scarcely breathing, each man moving forward at his own pace, apart and silent. The secret was patience, and it took three hours to position ourselves inside the ring of guard dogs, below the cliffs. The night, I remember, was warm, and the crickets active. Cyprus has a levantine odor to it. Maybe it is the smell of carob trees, or maybe the sage, but when I think of Cyprus I think of that aroma. We could hear the murmur of voices higher up, the click and clack of weaponry, unpacked and checked. Let it be, I remember thinking. We'll wait for them here.

"The sun had long set and the moon appeared. We waited lying flat on our fronts for, oh, maybe an hour. Waiting was familiar to us, listening to the darkness and the slight sounds of the lizards, studying the stars that are so bright and clear in Cyprus. Suddenly, the voices became louder. Footsteps, boots sliding on the rock face, quiet curses in Greek that could barely be distinguished. Wait, wait. Two men were descending, laden with boxes, trying to be quiet despite the difficult terrain and their heavy burdens. You could hear their heavy breathing.

"They were twenty yards away. 'Halt! *Stamata! Dur!*' We were obliged to call this out before firing. By the time you shouted out, it could be too late. But calling out could stop the hot-headed from opening fire out of impatience or fright. 'Halt! *Stamata! Dur!*' I shouted again. It sounded commanding and threatening, not really how I felt, I assure you. I stood up, my Sterling cocked. The man in front stopped dead in his tracks, surprised and shocked. From up above a burst of automatic gunfire skittered and zipped among the rock and scrub. I hit the ground and gave the order to fire. We kept our heads down, firing blind. I remember thinking 'that was lucky, the bloody Sterling hasn't jammed this time.' Those old subma-chine guns always made me nervous. They worked at whim, sending bullets zinging in a dozen directions.

"Our fire seemed to last an eternity, but it was probably only a few seconds. Carefully, I raised my head. Silence. Then a groan from yards away. More silence. I demanded a surren-der. Nothing. Miller went with three men up the steep track to the first cave to flush out the automatic. We covered them as they moved quietly up the cliff. Moments of tension. But nothing. Nobody was there. Spirited away.

"That night we captured two large boxes, one containing weapons, the other ammunition, but the men got away. All but one, who had been hit twice—once in the left arm, once in the head. We improvised a crude stretcher and carried the young EOKA fighter back through the moonlit countryside to the truck. Hidden among the bushes, it was so skillfully cam-ouflaged that even we had trouble working out in the night where we had left it. Our prisoner was unconscious and bleed-ing, and we worried about getting him back to camp and find-ing a medical orderly in time. I dared not break radio silence, and it took two hours to get back to camp.

"The injured man was whisked out that night from our camp in a helicopter, almost within minutes of our arrival. I'll say this for the medics, they were bloody good. For him it was the main hospital in Nicosia and, if he lived, interrogation. We never saw him again. We had put one terrorist out of com-mission and had captured arms and ammunition. The Com-manding Officer was pleased. End of story, as far as I was concerned. Funny about people's priorities, though. I was sent back to the caves with my men to recover the bullet casings. Ambushes are one thing, litter another."

"That was bloody dangerous," said Richard. "Glad my National Service wasn't that active!"

"But that's not the end of the story," said Gerald. "In the mid-eighties I was visiting a supplier outside London about a contract. Looking at myself in the car mirror I realized I needed a haircut. Civilians expect soldiers to look like soldiers. So as I drove through a London suburb, I spotted a barbershop and parked the car. The shop was empty, and I sat down in the chair, inspecting my state of grooming in the mirror. The barber had a handsome, open face, a shock of white hair, and a trimmed moustache, which reminded me of pictures of Colonel Grivas of EOKA. He wore a collarless white shirt and baggy, unpressed trousers, a bit reminiscent of a hadji in a Turkish village. I hadn't thought of Cyprus for years. The only thing that reminded me of it was an attachment to my General Service Medal, which simply read 'Cyprus' and which was hidden somewhere at the bottom of a drawer.

"The usual pleasantries, weather, traffic, all that.

"'Just my luck,' said the barber. 'It's always nice weather in London when I go on holiday.'

"'Where are you going?' I asked.

"'My home town,' he replied.

"'Which is where?'

"'Cyprus. I'm Cypriot, but I've been here for thirty years.'

"'I've always made it a practice never to be too forthcoming with strangers about my military service. You never know what mental baggage they're carrying around. I remember being alone in a railway carriage with an attractive young girl on the way to Norwich once. After a brief conversation, she suddenly burst out, 'Why can't you bloody well leave us alone, and go back to your own bloody country?' She was Irish and I was stationed in Belfast at the time. I'll never forget that; you don't expect it in a railway carriage.

"So this time I asked, 'Which part?'

"'A village in the Panhandle.'

"'The Karpass?' I asked.

"There was an awkward silence. I saw him inspecting me, trying to work something out. I eyed his barber's razor and thought about lines of retreat. You never know these days.

"'Yialousa,' was all he said.

"Immediately, I knew. Yes, he was middle-aged, but it was Spirou, in Hounslow of all places. Amazing! You couldn't make up a story like this. Thirty years later and two thousand miles away, or whatever?

"'So you remember me bringing the men to get their hair cut on a Thursday morning?'

"'Bloody right, I remember it,' said Spirou. He still had a slight guttural twinge to his voice, but his English was excellent. 'Doing business with the enemy gave me endless problems.'

"'Come on, Spirou, we were good fun. A few laughs, a few jokes. Couldn't have been all that bad.'

"'I needed the money, so did my father. But the villagers were jealous. The export of olives and oranges had dried up. Times were hard.'

"'Beautiful island,' I said. 'Tragic really. You have ruins from every civilization in the Middle East. You have a fabulous climate, wonderful beaches. But look at the political mess. Tell me, whatever happened to Ariadne?'

"Spirou laid down his electric razor and his comb and went to the door. 'Come here a moment, love. We have a visitor.'

"From the rear of the premises came a woman, stout in the way of older peasant women, dressed head to toe in black, Cypriot style. She wore a lace collar around her neck and her long graying hair was caught firmly in a bun at the back of her head. Handsome, with a twinkle in her eye. It was the eyes that gave her away.

"'Ariadne. Meet an old acquaintance. Now I've forgotten your name.'

"Well, why should he remember after all those years? The only reason I remembered names from Yialousa myself was, well, it's difficult to put some things out of your mind. I told him my name.

"'This is Gerald. Do you remember him? He used to bring his men to get their hair cut? He was a troop commander at Akrades.'

"'Mr. Gerald, nice to see you. But what are you doing here?'

"'I could ask you the same question,' I said. 'You had competition in the old days, Spirou. There wasn't a man at Akrades who wouldn't have walked over broken glass for this charming lady. It's a pleasure to meet you at last. So, how did you both end up here, in Hounslow?'

"'I followed him.'

"'So you didn't marry in Cyprus?'

"'No, much later.'

"'Tell me,' I said.

"Spirou began. 'Yialousa was a small community, and everyone did his bit for *enosis* in those days. It was a noble cause, until the leadership went too far and provoked the Turks beyond endurance. Idiots! I did my bit, with Ari, Ariadne's brother. We used to smuggle in munitions through Kilanemos, the fishing village up the coast, and distribute them around. At first, just around the Karpass peninsula, but later, when the British paras interrupted distribution in the Troodos Mountains, we covered the northern part of the island as well. It was dangerous work.

"'Then we realized that you British were watching Kilanemos. One night you invaded the village and turned all the old women out of their beds, hands up against the wall in their nightclothes, dying of fright. Some of your officers were real hotheads! No idea about public relations. We always knew we would win.

"'Anyway, we then arranged a shipment through Ayios Simeon and met the couriers in some caves outside the town. We unpacked and checked the goods and then left the couriers with an automatic to cover our escape. Two teams headed to the west. Ari and I were descending the cliffs when we were ambushed by a British patrol. A voice shouted "Halt! *Stamata! Dur!*" Ari was ahead of me, about five paces, and yelled, "Run for it!"

"'It was nighttime, and although the moon was out, I thought the British soldiers would never hit us in the dark. They weren't known for being sharpshooters. But I abandoned the guns and ammunition and ran like hell, zig-zagging away from them down the hill and thanking God I was wearing gloves so the firearms and boxes would be free of fingerprints. The couriers were firing, covering my back. But where was Ari? I was unarmed and I dared not stop.'

"Ariadne filled in. 'He saved his own life and abandoned Ari to the British, to be taken off and tortured. I loved him, but I couldn't understand how he could abandon my brother. He had rifles, bullets, even a mortar among the arms for distribution. And he ran. At least, that's how it appeared.

"'From that time, nobody in the village would speak to Spirou. EOKA blackballed him, and nobody visited the barbershop. He was treated like a traitor, an outcast, but weekly he would come to my house.

"'He would say, "Ariadne, I love you. I had no choice with Ari. Marry me and come away from this place." You always pull the blanket over onto your side, as we Greeks say. That was his story.

"'Every week I would say, "Find my brother and then we can talk." This went on for many months. Constantly rejected, but always determined, he never gave up.'

"Spirou rose and paced the floor as he continued. 'Nobody knew what had happened to Ari. A shepherd friend of mine drove his flock up the hillside by the caves but found no sign of him or the rifles and rounds we had been carrying. No one from Ayios Simeon had seen Ari and we got no information from the British. I was beside myself with panic and grief. I got a friend to make inquiries at Akrades, and contacted my Turkish friend, Aziz, but he found out nothing. I phoned the local RAF stations, the local hospitals, the orange wholesaler down in Famagusta, anyone who could give me a lead. Total silence. A blanket of fog had come down over Ari.

"'When independence came in 1959, my father and I hoped the villagers would forgive and forget. In Cyprus, time is everything. We arranged for a four-piece band and trestle tables in front of the church. We hung garlands and colored streamers across the square. It was expensive. Father did it for me. It used up much of his savings. The priest contributed some ouzo and commanderia, and we waited for the celebrations to start. But nobody came, not even the village mukhtar who my father had grown up with, his best friend. It was then that I decided to come to England.' Spirou looked at Ariadne.

"'The village was poisoned,' she said. 'The fighting with the British and the Turks and the bitter feelings about Spirou had sapped the spirit of community. People avoided their former friends. I left to attend a nurse's training course in Nicosia and afterwards went to work in a nursing home for the chronically ill. Some had polio, others had terminal cancer. I worked there for several weeks before I was assigned to the ward at the top of the building that accommodated young men who had been gravely injured during the communal disturbances. Whether Greeks or Turks, they were largely forgotten. Apparently, this is quite common after a war,' she looked at me for understanding. 'People turn their backs on disabled veterans, as if wanting to forget and start afresh.' I thought of the two world wars.

"'A particular young man immediately attracted my attention. He was silent and brooding, apparently seeing and hearing nothing, lost in a catatonic state. I felt a mixture of exhilaration and horror. It was unmistakably Ari, my brother. Fortune had led me to him. I threw my arms around him and wept and laughed, but he did not respond. It seems a bullet had damaged a nerve. A British surgeon had operated and seemed confident of his recovery. He thought Ari could expect some degree of paralysis down his right side, but would recover his speech. That was three years before.

"'There then began a long and painful period of care. I managed to persuade the nursing home to leave me on the ward, on the principle that Ari might recover if I, his sister, were caring for him. At first there was no response, and he just sat impassively in a wheelchair for most of the day. Then gradually, little flickers of interest appeared on his face, first in response to a television program about animals, then in reaction to an ice cream brought to him by a visiting cousin. At last, after months of sitting with him, talking about childhood events and people, it happened. A puzzled look came over his face, and he uttered the start of the word I had been waiting for, "Aria. . . ."

"'From that moment, he progressed rapidly, learning again to speak and to use his eyes and his memory. A baby in his mid-twenties. Slowly the memories came back, and the use of his hands, so that I no longer had to spoon-feed him.

"'Then one day Ari told me, haltingly and with many pauses, what had happened at Ayios Simeon. Spirou had been carrying the guns and Ari the ammunition, so Spirou was effectively unarmed, as he had claimed all along. But Spirou was also carrying a list of EOKA leaders and distribution points. It would have been death to the movement had this list been captured. Both Ari and Spirou knew the list must be safeguarded at all costs. Spirou could have torn it up, or, better, swallowed it. It was only a piece of paper, after all. But that sort of thing is for spy novels. In reality he had no time to think of such a plan, much less to carry it out, so he ran.

"'Back in the village he could tell nobody the truth about the arms shipment and the secret list. We believed at the time that there were British spies in every village. Only later we understood how little information the British had. We kept our mouths shut or risked being arrested by the British or tortured by the Turks. Only weeks before, Turks from a nearby village took a young Greek and burned his body in the village square. Ari had shouted, "Run for it!" and Spirou had escaped with the list.

"'Three months later I came to London, and Spirou and I were married in the Greek Orthodox church in West London. Some of our Cypriot friends came to the wedding, but no one from Yialousa.'

"'We later brought Ari to London, where we could look after him,' added Spirou. 'He's partly paralyzed and often confused. He has trouble remembering things. The doctors have tried, but he hasn't made much progress. It's a joyless life. And all because he believed in *enosis*.'

"I saw a glint of anger in Spirou's eyes as he added, 'I wish I could get my hands on the bastard who shot him.'

"I remembered the warm night air of Ayios Simeon, the crickets, the murmur of voices, the approaching footsteps, and my finger closing around the cold steel of the trigger.

"I kept my composure, smiled in a noncommittal manner, and busily rifled my wallet for a suitable banknote. I paid Spirou for the haircut and bid the once beautiful Ariadne farewell.

"As I stepped out into the noonday sun, I breathed a sigh of relief. I don't know how long I sat in the car before moving on."

We stayed in La Storta and went to bed early. The next day we rose at four A.M., hoping to traverse the major part of the route into Rome before the noise and fumes of the morning rush hour quelled our spirits. On the approach, we spotted St. Peter's dome in the distance and then lost it from sight as we entered Rome via the Flamina bridge, traditionally crossed by triumphant generals. We passed again over the Tiber on the fourth-century Ponte Milvio and soon found ourselves walking into the magnificence of St. Peter's Square.

Epilogue

Chaucer never wrote an epilogue,
Perhaps exhausted by his dialogue.
But we add one to our much lighter fare,
To mark arrival in Saint Peter's Square.
Eleven hundred miles are now complete,
A tribute to our backbone—and our feet!
Though blistered, weary, we cannot repress
A feeling of achievement and success.

And waiting at the airport we exchange
Our e-mail details. And some may arrange
To meet, to study photos, and reflect
On wines and meals and jokes they recollect.
Ah! Lucky and indulged they are indeed
These modern characters, this lucky breed
Of educated people who aspire
To better ways of living, then retire
With health and money till some distant time,
When body functions are in overtime!

But do we differ truly from before,
From some unnamed, obscure progenitor?
No! Though science brings so many changes,
The gamut of man's foolish folly ranges
As widely as it ever did of old,
When Chaucer's moral stories once were told.

Still here is *fear,* not far behind is *lust,*
Cash to the *wicked,* unfairness to the *just.*
Here we have *envy,* everywhere *is greed;*
Vice and *corruption* with all the others breed.

But! F*aith's* among us, also *charity,*
Forgiveness too (for our verbosity!).
Kindness? Compassion? Still in evidence.
Credit for *virtue, patience* for the dense.
Integrity as always still survives,
And *selflessness* and *trust* enhance our lives.
So though we've lost 'the varray, parfit knight'
There still are those who know their wrong from right.
No, don't *despair* nor act the misanthrope,
Where there is *love,* forever there is *hope.*

Accept this tribute, ringing in your ears,
In honor, Chaucer, of your six hundred years.
Ah! Chaucer! How the childhood memories last
Of English lessons now forever past,
Of torturous scribbling on the Summoner's Tale,
Of prologues, pilgrimage and Tabard ale.
And how the aging, fickle memory lingers
Of Middle English and of inky fingers!
The pedagogue who gleefully assigns
This noble poet's half-remembered lines
For homework on a sunny summer's day,
When monks and shipmen are a world away,
"Discuss the Pardoner; furthermore, review

Epilogue

The several ways you're able to construe
The Pardoner a hypocrite to be.
By Monday morning, hand it into me."
Oh, happy days, put nearly out of mind,
Except for those who, grumbling, come behind,
Still learning lines and trying to understand
Your medieval mirror on the land.

You critics, literati, modern sages,
Flipping idly through our modest pages,
Judge us gently, for the love of rhyme,
Has much declined since peerless Chaucer's time.
Will Chaucer still be taught in English Lit.
A generation hence or will schools quit,
Abandon classics, let their students cram
On airport fiction for a school exam?
Rarely since entertainment first began
Have humans shown such short attention span.
Nor have we helped when, well-advised, we chose
To forego Chaucer's verse and write in prose.
Yet think on this, if you be unenthused,
Geoffrey himself would surely be amused.

And so we leave you, reader, homeward bound.
And though these tales be not deep-laid, profound,
Let others better tales recount in rhyme,
If they can find the impulse and the time.